*To living, laughing, and learning
under the sea.*

———

For further information, contact:
Tumblehome, Inc.
201 Newbury St, Suite 201
Boston, MA 02116
http://tumblehomebooks.org/

Library of Congress Control Number 2022942181
ISBN-13 978-1-943431-80-9
ISBN-10 1-943431-80-9

Prager, Ellen
Escape Undersea / Ellen Prager - 1st ed
Illustrated by Tammy Yee

Printed in Taiwan

10 9 8 7 6 5 4 3 2 1

TUMBLEHOME, Inc.

Escape Undersea

Book Three of
The Wonder List Adventures

Ellen Prager

Illustrated by Tammy Yee

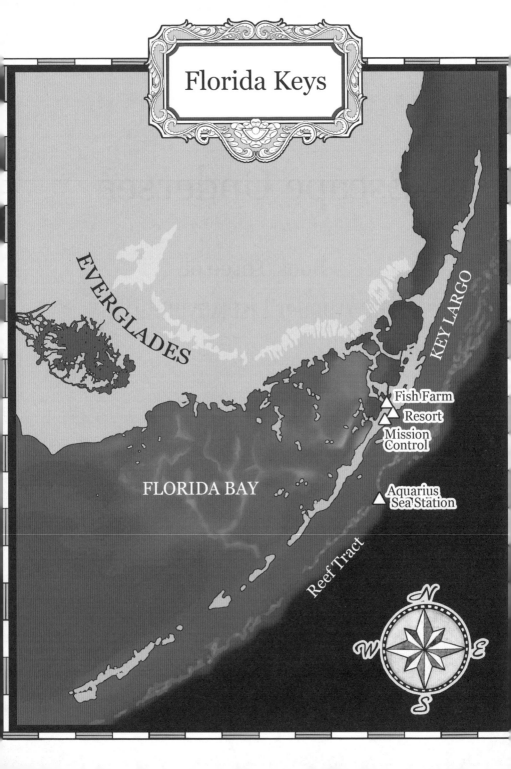

Florida Keys

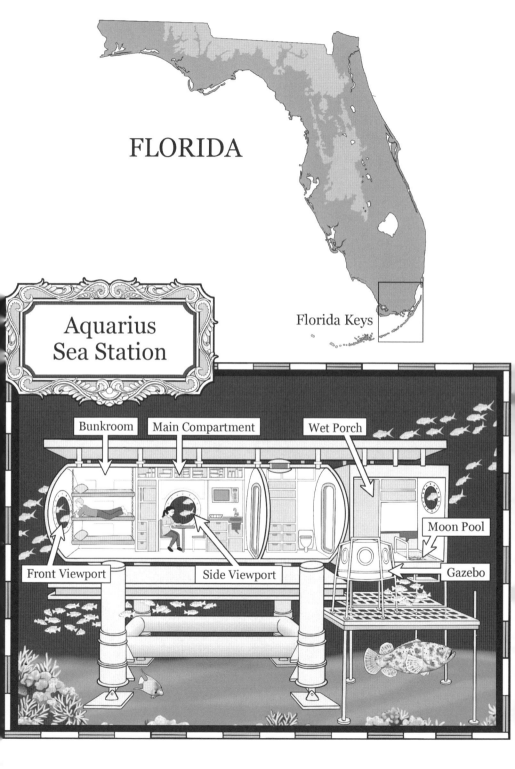

CONTENTS

Prologue

A Burial at Sea

U*nhooked Fish Farm,* Key Largo, Florida
      The young man and boy stood somberly on the dock staring into the water of the canal. To their left was a boat ramp. To their right, the canal opened into Florida Bay—a wedge-shaped body of water linked to the sea and divided into numerous basins by a network of mudbanks and mangrove islands.

Black corkscrew curls fell over the forehead of the mocha-skinned young man as he looked down at the boy. "You ready?"

Wiry and pale, the boy wiped a bead of sweat from his brow and nodded. He gazed into the water-filled bucket sitting between them. The six fish inside floated still at the surface.

"Do you want to say anything?"

The boy pursed his lips and scrunched up his face in thought. He smoothed his t-shirt and board shorts before pulling his baseball cap snug. "What do people usually say?"

The young man shrugged. "I don't know. Something about how they lived a good life and would be at peace I guess."

"You say it," the boy said.

"Okay. They were... uh... pretty fish, ate a lot, but lived a short life."

"How long do they usually live?"

"Not sure. Now return to the sea where you belong and hopefully no one will eat you."

The hint of a smile appeared on the boy's face.

"You want to do the honors?"

The boy picked up the bucket and gently dumped it into the water beside the dock. "Bye, fish. Sorry you died."

The two watched as the fish bobbed up and down before drifting down the canal.

"Back to work, I guess," said the young man as he turned to walk away.

The boy followed.

A sudden splashing sound drew their attention. They wheeled around.

"Hey, where'd the fish go?" asked the boy.

"That's weird," returned the young man. "I don't see them."

"Maybe something ate them."

"Maybe."

*   *   *

Back to the Moon Pool

O *ne year later.*
  Above, the water was green. Not just a little or slightly green, but shockingly green and almost thick. Ezzy stopped her ascent and hovered below the goopy discolored water. It reminded her of pea soup. The idea of eating pea soup was disgusting, swimming through it was worse. A total nightmare. Ezzy hated nightmares. She sometimes had them about being chased by lava or trapped in an ice cave. Unfortunately, her nightmares were a lot like memories from the last two years. She had thought this year would be better. Even so, Ezzy stayed on the lookout for what could go wrong—like having to swim through gross goopy pea soup water. She nearly revisited lunch in her SCUBA regulator. Instead, she breathed in and exhaled slowly like she'd been taught.

As Ezzy stared at the green goop overhead, something grabbed her leg. She jerked away while simultaneously looking down. Hovering below was the safety diver accompanying her to the surface. He nodded upward, shook his head and pointed to the blue depths below. Ezzy stared at him questioningly. She and her younger brother, Luke, were supposed to go directly to the surface. No stops. No diversions. The diver pointed downward more insistently. Ezzy saw Luke beneath them already headed back down.

Putting her finger to her thumb, fourteen-year-old Ezzy Skylar gave the diver the okay sign. She tugged the string on the relief valve of her buoyancy compensator. A cluster of air bubbles floated upward and Ezzy sank slightly. Following the safety diver, she rolled over and kicked, heading down. She watched the depth on her dive computer. Twenty feet. Twenty-five feet. Thirty feet. Thirty-five feet.

Ezzy knew where they were headed but didn't understand why. If she and Luke stayed down much longer and then went up without going through decompression, they could get gas bubbles in their blood, which cause the bends. It was also known as decompression sickness—and it could be deadly. Ezzy's heartbeat quickened as she wondered if the icky pea-soup water at the surface had caused their sudden change in plans.

A long silver fish darted past. Ezzy again jerked back. The fish was nearly four feet in length and with its mouth agape she could see its teeth—lots and lots of stiletto sharp teeth. Ezzy recognized it—barracuda.

She eyed the toothy barracuda now floating nearby and swore the fish stared back. Ezzy's heart raced as bubbles erupted from her regulator. She'd gotten a lot better about not freaking out around wild animals, especially those with sharp claws or teeth. And ever since Ezzy had done her first dives while learning to SCUBA, she'd discovered a new sense of calm and peace in the quiet of the underwater world. But being in a staring contest with a sharp-toothed barracuda was pushing her new sense of calm and bravery to its limits.

The safety diver swam closer, stopped, and pointedly gave Ezzy the okay sign. She consciously slowed her breathing and returned the hand signal, remembering what their dive instructor had told them. Barracuda are territorial, super curious, and often follow divers around but rarely bite anyone. Ezzy wondered what the instructor's definition of "rarely" was. She conceded the staring contest to the sleek silvery fish and again descended toward the seafloor.

Headed down, Ezzy turned hesitantly to look back. The barracuda was about a foot from her fins, following her like a predator on the prowl. She took a deep calming breath and silently repeated the mantra she'd started on her first SCUBA dive in the ocean: *I am not good fish food. I am not good fish food.*

Seconds later, a school of yellow and silver snappers zipped by. Ezzy recognized them from earlier in the day. Behind the snappers trailed a pair of larger triangular black and yellow fish. Then came a school of plump turquoise fish with patches of yellow and pink. Their surprisingly big buckteeth gave them away. Parrotfish. Luke had told her that their name came from their beak-shaped mouths.

More fish streamed by. It was like an undersea conga line. With a poke, the safety diver urged Ezzy to keep moving. She kicked slowly downward while looking to see where the fish were coming from. It was the coral reef about twenty feet away. Earlier, when they'd swum down from the surface, a ton of fish had been swimming around the reef. Some had cruised among the bumpy brown and greenish mounds or heads of coral. Others had hovered under large plate-like coral overhangs. And above the undulating surface of the reef had been clouds of small blue fish and frilly black fish that rose and sank in synchrony. But the only fish in sight now were headed away, as if the reef's residents were evacuating. *Did it have something to do with the pea soup water overhead?*

In the distance beyond the ridge-like reef, Ezzy could see only a vast blueness. But then, at the very edge of her vision, she thought she saw something move. Something dark and big. Really big. Ezzy stopped kicking. She concentrated, peering into the distance. Were the shadows undersea playing tricks on her or was there something out there? The safety diver tapped her leg and again waved her downward. Ezzy glanced back beyond the reef. All she saw was an empty expanse of blue.

Ezzy turned her attention downward, telling herself that it was probably just the weird things light did underwater. Like when she was learning to dive, and her SCUBA instructor nicked his leg seventy feet down. Blood had dripped down his leg and Ezzy nearly freaked out. It was blue-green! Like alien blood. Her instructor later explained that in the ocean, long-waved red light is absorbed first. So, at about sixty feet and deeper, without artificial light, you can't see red. Things that are red, like blood, appear blue-green. Still freaky, Ezzy thought.

Soon their destination came into view and Ezzy forgot all about alien blood or what she might have seen beyond the reef. Within the ocean's azure depths, the large yellow structure below appeared otherworldly. It was the Aquarius Sea Station—the world's only undersea research laboratory.

The yellow sea station sat above the white sandy seafloor atop four long cylindrical metal legs. The main portion of the undersea lab was also a cylinder about ten feet in diameter and about the length of a mobile home. On the side and front were big round viewports and at the back was a square section called the wet porch that housed the moon pool—the open hatchway into the lab. Attached nearby was a white gazebo-like metal structure. Patches of colorful growth covered much of the station. Clumps of bright orange cup coral intermingled with green and purple encrustations. Yellow tube sponge stuck out at one corner and green whiplike growths hung down from the top.

The safety diver veered off to the side and waved Ezzy ahead. In front of her, Luke's fins disappeared as he swam under the structure and into the moon pool. Ezzy followed, swimming under the overlying deck. The top of her SCUBA tank bumped the metal overhead. Ezzy shook her head. Even underwater she was clumsy. If only she'd stop growing. Ezzy was still the tallest in her classes. She hoped that no one had noticed her tank hit.

Seconds later, she was in the moon pool. It was a shallow rectangular opening to the sea at the far end of the wet porch compartment, which was a room with metal walls about the size of her bedroom at home. The water in the moon pool was only about two and a half feet deep. Sliding in next to Luke, Ezzy knelt on the metal grating floor and popped her head up into the air above.

Luke spit out his regulator. "I thought we had to go up?"

Ezzy shook her head and shrugged while removing the regulator from her mouth.

"No need to worry," said a voice from above.

Taking off her mask, Ezzy looked up. Otter, the surprisingly large, bearded habitat technician they'd met earlier, stared down at them. He reminded her of a hairy white version of a famous ex-wrestler turned movie star. "I thought we had to go up right away," she repeated.

Otter smiled reassuringly. "We've got a little time.

We always leave a buffer, just in case. You're good for about another fifteen minutes."

"Then what?" asked Luke.

Otter scratched his beard. Beneath his Aquarius Station t-shirt, the man's overly large bicep bulged. "Well, my friend, if you don't hit the surface in the next fifteen minutes or so, looks like you'll be sleeping with the fishes. And I mean that literally."

Luke's eyes got wide.

Otter winked. "Not in the bad concrete-block tied to your ankles way like in the movies."

"Won't we have to go through decompression then?" Ezzy asked.

A well-lined tanned face topped by short spiky white hair appeared at the moon pool railing. "No need to fret about that just yet, young Ezzy."

Otter strode away from the moon pool. "Hang out right there for a bit while I confer with folks topside."

Phil Smith, the man at the railing, was joined by his wife, Gracie. They had been living in the undersea lab for almost a week and were the ones that had invited the Skylars to visit. Like her husband, Gracie was in her seventies but still had an athletic build along with spiky white hair. When she smiled, the lines around her bright blue eyes crinkled, exuding an infectious joy. "Hey," she said.

"Why'd we come back?" Luke questioned.

"Not sure," Phil replied.

With a look of disgust, Ezzy asked, "Was it the pea soup water?"

"Pea soup water?" Gracie inquired.

"Yeah," Luke said. "Super green goopy water near the surface."

"I think that's why we turned around and came back," Ezzy added. "And lots of fish were swimming away from the reef."

Gracie paused and stared at her husband before saying, "We saw some fish through the viewport headed under the station. But that's normal. It's like an artificial reef and a lot of fish hang out there."

But Ezzy wasn't so sure it was normal. Something felt wrong. Her father would probably say she was being too quick to assume the worst. Since their adventures in the Galápagos and Greenland, she'd developed a habit of deciding that whenever something a bit unusual or unexpected happened, it was part of an evil scheme. Someone bad doing something evil or malicious. While driving to one of their SCUBA classes at home, they'd gotten a flat tire. Ezzy had wondered if someone had slashed it to prevent them from getting certified or something. Her father pointed to the nail they'd driven over and assured her it was simply bad luck. She wasn't so sure.

Ezzy knelt in the water of the moon pool contemplating the pea soup water at the surface. Had someone caused or created it on purpose? How? Why? Had they stumbled onto another evil-bad-guy-scheme? Or had the adventures of the last two years made her overly suspicious, affected her way of thinking?

Next thing Ezzy knew she was tumbling over underwater. Something big and heavy had slammed into her, pushing her over. Ezzy twisted around to look back. An enormous fish now hovered in her place. It was bigger than she was, fat, a mottled tannish green, with a huge mouth and large protruding eyes. Ezzy watched it nervously as she scooted back to her knees, keeping away from the fish's gigantic mouth. Another similarly humongous fish swam up and sidled more gently up to Luke.

"Uh, guys," Ezzy stuttered. "There's two really big fish down here."

Above, Otter had returned and chuckled. "That's just Gertrude and Gandolf, our resident goliath groupers. They like to hang out with us."

Gracie laughed. "They especially *love* to hang out with Otter."

He shrugged. "What can I say? I'm lovable, even to the fish."

Phil Smith shook his head. "Yeah, they have a new policy down here. No hugging or groping of the groupers. It's tempting but touching them can wipe off their protective mucus. It's not good for them."

Ezzy rolled her eyes. "This thing is big enough to open its mouth and suck us in. Hugging is not an option."

Luke smiled. "I like them."

"You would," Ezzy responded, feeling relieved. It was probably one of the giant fish that she'd seen earlier behind the reef.

The two groupers shifted closer to Luke. Then, almost reluctantly, they glided away. Ezzy noticed Luke drifting with them as if he was going to follow the fish.

"No, you don't," she said, grabbing the top of his tank and hauling him back into the moon pool. She shook her head thinking: after their previous adventures she'd become braver but also more wary, whereas her brother had become more reckless. She'd have to keep a sharp eye on him.

The two safety divers popped up where the fish had been.

"Hey, guys," said one before turning to Otter. "What's happening?"

"Zhao, do you want the good or bad news first?"

"Uh... good?"

"The team up top are sending down full-face masks so you and Lola, can go back up."

"What's the bad news?"

"Well," Otter said before pausing to look at Ezzy and Luke. "I guess it depends on your perspective. You two are about to become the youngest aquanauts ever. At least for the night."

"Really?" Luke asked.

"Really," he answered. "There's an unusual and

extensive algae bloom at the surface. We're not sure if it's safe to swim through with regular SCUBA gear. And you two." He again stared pointedly at Ezzy and Luke. "Are not trained on a full-face rig. Safer to spend the night down here and hopefully in the morning the bloom will have drifted off or dissipated so you can go up on regular gear."

Gracie clapped her hands. "Oh honey pie, it'll be an underwater sleepover."

"Right you are, my undersea angel," responded Phil.

Otter shook his head and smiled. "You two are seriously narced." He turned to Ezzy and Luke. "That's short for nitrogen narcosis. When you've been down here for twenty-four hours or more, your body becomes saturated with gas and much of it is nitrogen, kinda like nitrous oxide, also known as laughing gas. *Some* people go a little loopy."

Ezzy chuckled. "Nah, they're always like that." Phil and Gracie Smith had not changed a bit since she'd first met them two summers ago in the Galápagos Islands. At first, she'd thought they were an elderly slow-moving couple with a tendency for ridiculous pet names and syrupy sugar-coated conversation. They ended up saving her and the others on their ship from being blown up. The pair were ex-military, totally lovable, and liked to play up the aging and infirm thing.

Gracie nodded. "Now come on up here, you two, and let's get you inside."

"The fast rescue boat is on its way out with sup- plies," Otter told them.

Ezzy and Luke took off their buoyancy compensa- tors and tanks and hung them on a rack next to the moon pool. They handed their masks and fins to Otter before climbing up the ladder into the wet porch com- partment of the sea station. The pair then peeled off their silver-striped, black wetsuits and dunked them in a bucket of soapy water. Otter rinsed the wetsuits and hung them up to dry. As they'd done earlier on their visit to the undersea station to see Phil and Gracie Smith, Ezzy and Luke rinsed in a freshwater shower.

Ezzy toweled off her ponytail and the shoulder- length strands of brown hair that had escaped. She glanced at Luke in his bathing suit drying off. She couldn't help but notice that he'd grown over the last year and lost some of his pudginess. He was still a little plump, freckled, with short blondish hair. Luke wasn't as tall as Ezzy yet, but he was catching up. Ezzy had her father's brown hair and thick eyebrows, along with his tall, thin stature. She wondered if her brother would grow up to look more like their mother with blonde curls and an athletic build. She thought they'd both gotten their mother's eyes—hazel with a touch of green. Her father liked to joke that her eyes sparkled with curiosity while Luke's held mostly love for ani- mals and more recently, a penchant for mischief.

By the time they were ready to enter the main compartment of the lab, another diver had arrived. He wore a mask that was connected to the hose from his air tank and covered his entire face. The diver delivered similar gear to Zhao and Lola, along with a large, covered metal pot. Otter took the pot, turned a valve to release the air inside, and undid the cover's clamps. Inside were supplies, including dry clothes for Ezzy and Luke. Using the full-face masks they'd received, Zhao and Lola followed the other diver out of the moon pool and headed for the surface.

Phil and Gracie Smith waved before returning to the main compartment. Otter showed Ezzy a lever by the sliding door between the compartments. "Pull this to the right and the hydraulic door opens. To the left, it closes. I'll slip inside to give you two some privacy to change."

Ezzy nodded as he left. She and Luke turned their backs to one another to remove their bathing suits and put on dry clothes.

"Ready?" Ezzy asked Luke.

"Always," he answered with a smirk.

Ezzy rolled her eyes and pulled the lever to the right. The door to the dry part of the station silently slid open. Luke jauntily stepped through. Before following, Ezzy glanced back at the moon pool.

She was amazed that the rectangular hatchway into the wet porch could remain open fifty feet down and water didn't flow in. Otter had explained earlier that they kept the air pressure inside the station equal to the seawater pressure outside, which was nearly two times that at the surface due to all the water overhead. This prevented the ocean from flowing in. If for some reason the air pressure started to fall inside the sea station (not good), the seawater would begin to rise inside the moon pool. Ezzy tried to memorize the exact level of the seawater in the hatchway. Not that she expected the ocean to start flooding in or anything, but weird things seem to happen around her and Luke. Better to keep an eye out for what could go wrong, especially when it was something that could lead to an exceptionally unpleasant and very wet situation inside the undersea lab. Potential drowning while fifty feet underwater trapped inside a metal cylinder on the seafloor was not something she wanted to experience— ever. It would be even worse than swimming through thick pea soup water. She again wondered what or who could have caused the strange algae bloom.

*   *   *

A Pretty Fish

The hydraulic door between the wet porch and dry portion of the sea station had closed behind Luke. Ezzy figured they must have shut it from the inside for some reason, or maybe it automatically closed each time someone passed through. She pulled the lever. The door slid open and Ezzy stepped through. A large rubbery green sea monster head popped up in front of her.

"Ahhhh!" Ezzy screamed leaping back.

Pulling off the creature-from-the-black-lagoon mask, Phil Smith smiled. "Couldn't resist."

Nearby, Luke bent over laughing. He sank to the floor. "Ha, ha, ha... that was *so* good."

Ezzy composed herself and made a squinty-eyed mad face at her twelve-year-old brother. Seconds later, she broke into a smile. "Okay, that was a good one."

"Come on in, honey," said Gracie. "And welcome back to your temporary home amid the fishes."

Once inside, Ezzy felt a sense of déjà vu. Earlier that day, when she and Luke had first entered the undersea lab, she could hardly believe they were there—inside the world's only undersea research laboratory. The invitation from Phil and Gracie Smith had come several months earlier, when the Skylars' trip to Australia's Great Barrier Reef (number three on Ezzy's deceased mother's Wonder List) had been cancelled due to a pandemic sweeping the world. Traveling halfway across the globe was out. But the Smiths had been asked to be part of a team of "aquanauts" living underwater to study the surrounding coral reefs and investigate the effects of living underwater on people of advanced age—Gracie and Phil Smith.

Dr. Skylar, Ezzy and Luke's father, decided that, with some precautions and testing along with a class to get SCUBA certified, it would be a great diversion from the world of virtual classes, virtual friends, and waiting for things to return to normal. Thankfully, by the time the Skylar family had finished their in-pool training, vaccines had become widely available, and the pandemic was waning. They had headed to the Florida Keys to do the required open-water dives for certification. Three days and several dives later, while accompanied by two safety divers, Ezzy and Luke had descended fifty feet to make a short visit to the undersea station. Unfortunately, due to a sinus infection, their father was unable to make the dive.

During their forty-five minutes in the laboratory, Ezzy and Luke had been given a tour, watched the undersea world through the viewports, learned about life in the station, and had a Zoom call with their father at mission control onshore.

Now, Ezzy and Luke were back inside the sea station, and this time for an overnight stay. Ezzy stared at the interior of the undersea lab. A long narrow aisle ran the length of its three main compartments. One section was mostly for science equipment and experiments. Another housed the kitchen. If you could call a hot water maker, microwave, sink and a drying rack a kitchen. Food supplies were stored on overhead shelving and in a minuscule refrigerator. A small metal table with bench seats sat beside one of the big round viewports.

One side or wall in the main compartment was covered with digital readouts and controls for the life support and communication systems. Ezzy had learned that they had two of everything so that if something broke, they always had a spare. The last compartment was the bunkroom, with two tiers of three bunks. Even before, when there were only five people in the lab, Ezzy had thought it was a small living space. "It's gonna be kinda tight in here with us here too."

"You hardly add anything," said Gracie. "It'll be cozy."

"Sugar plum," added her husband. "You always look on the bright side. A glass half full kind of gal."

Ezzy rolled her eyes but couldn't help but smile. They hadn't changed a bit.

"More like claustrophobic," said a stocky woman with ebony skin, sitting on a stool in front of a computer. "Why I agreed to this in the first place I'll never know."

As Otter slipped by in the narrow central aisleway, he patted the woman on the shoulder. "Because you have six to nine hours a day diving to 100 feet to study your precious corals and you can watch the data streaming live in here from all that gear you've got out there. That's why."

The woman shrugged. "True."

Luke turned to Otter. "Hey, where's the other guy, Drew?"

Otter pointed to the big viewport at the far end of the laboratory. Outside the window stretched a long yellow hose. "He's out cleaning and inspecting the viewport. This morning we found some unusual scrape marks in the acrylic."

"Unusual scrape marks?" Ezzy asked.

"Probably nothing," said Otter quickly.

Ezzy made a mental note on the growing list of unusual things that had happened so far on their "quick visit" to the lab: pea-soup water, reef evacuation, and now strange scratch marks on a window. She then noticed a red and white striped fish with long frilly spines swimming in front of the viewport. "That's a pretty fish."

Seconds later, a spear shot through the fish. Ezzy recoiled as a hand popped up holding the spear, followed by a diver whose regulator was attached to the yellow hose.

"Nice shot!" said Otter.

"He killed it," groaned Ezzy.

"That's a lionfish," said Luke. "It's invasive. I read about them."

Figures, thought Ezzy. Luke reads and remembers everything.

"That's right," said Otter. "Around here, the only good lionfish is a dead lionfish. They belong in the Indian and Pacific Oceans, not here off Florida. Eat all the small fish and crustaceans, breed like crazy, and have no natural predators. And they have toxin in those pretty looking frilly spines. You do not want to get stuck by one of those. Luckily, they don't get much larger than about a foot long like the one Drew just got. But still, they are a threat to the reefs. And even small ones can be a bit aggressive."

"How'd they get here?" Ezzy asked.

Otter turned to Luke.

"Some people buy them for aquariums and when they get too big, they release them."

"Exactly," Otter said. "And during a hurricane, some got released from a damaged aquarium."

Holding up the speared lionfish, Drew waved to the group inside.

Ezzy and Luke waved back.

"Why don't you two have a seat," Otter told them. "We'll set up a call with your father and Dr. Juan, the base doctor. I want to be sure there are no medical issues I need to be aware of while you're here and for decompression."

"Decompression?" Ezzy said. "Do we have to go into that small chamber thing back at the base?"

Otter shook his head. "No, we do it right here in the comfort of the station. We close the hatch over the moon pool and then overnight we'll reduce the pressure inside so that by morning, it'll be the same as the surface and we can all swim up."

"All swim up?" questioned the scientist sitting by the computer. "But the mission's not over. I still have experiments out there and more data to collect."

"Sorry, Professor Miller," replied Otter. "Safety first. Not only do we need to get our young aquanauts back to the surface, but there's also a storm brewing in the Caribbean and the forecast track has it headed this way. Even if the kids weren't here, we'd have to cut the mission short and start decompression. I was going to break the bad news to you before dinner. Believe me, you do not want to be down here in a hurricane."

Otter's calm demeanor and confidence comforted Ezzy and made her think there probably wasn't anything to worry about. But in the back of her mind a hint of doubt lingered. Ezzy knew if she let it grow into worry it could lead to panic. She silently added *possible hurrricane* to her growing list of things-that-could-go-very-wrong underwater. Then said to herself, *no, I am the new brave Ezzy.*

"I waited a long time for this mission," moaned Professor Miller. "I still have data to collect, and what about all my equipment out on the reef?"

"Sorry Doc, but we need to get you out safely and prepare to batten down the hatches. In the morning, the divers will help collect your gear."

"These hurricanes don't always do what's forecasted," the scientist added. "Can't we wait and see before scrubbing the rest of the mission?"

"No can do," Otter replied.

*   *   *

Otter called mission control and readied for a Zoom connect with Ezzy and Luke's father and Dr. Juan. Ezzy and Luke sat at the table by the big viewport and stared out. A few silvery yellow snappers swam up, hovered, and appeared to watch them curiously.

"Ahh, Otter," stuttered Professor Miller. "I'm seeing some unusual readings from my gear on the reef."

"What sort of readings?"

"A steep drop in temperature at the deep reef and some unexpected fluctuations in the oxygen data."

"Maybe it has something to do with the green goop at the surface," suggested Luke.

Professor Miller scratched her head. "Possibly. I've got sensors deployed in the deep reef going up to about the top of the corals at around thirty feet. I'm looking mainly at changes in pH having to do with ocean acidification. As more carbon dioxide enters the atmosphere, more is being absorbed in the ocean. It's another aspect of climate change. The ocean is becoming more acidic."

Luke rolled his eyes. "Yeah, we know all about climate change. Have first-hand experience there."

Ezzy nodded, thinking back to their adventure in Greenland last summer.

"Well," said Professor Miller. "My sensors can also detect changes in temperature, oxygen, turbidity, and chlorophyll. I've got them cabled to the lab so that I can watch in real-time what's happening."

"What's turbidity?" asked Luke.

Before she could answer, the laptop on the table pinged and a Zoom call opened up. "Helloooo down there," said a voice through the computer.

Ezzy and Luke squeezed in together so they were on camera and could see their father.

"There are my little aquanaut fishes," said Dr. Skylar. "How are you doing? Ready for an underwater sleepover? You two will have a squid of a time."

"Squid of a time?" Otter questioned.

Luke laughed. "He means whale of a time."

"Oh, is that it?" chuckled Dr. Skylar.

"Any medical issues we need to know about before decompression?" Otter asked.

"No worries there," said Dr. Skylar. "I've already covered that with Dr. Juan. Those two are as healthy as an elephant."

"An elephant?" questioned Otter.

"He means horse," said Ezzy. "Healthy as a horse. Geez, Dad."

Dr. Skylar laughed. "Exactly."

Otter shook his head. "They'll be monitored overnight like the rest of us."

Gracie leaned into the picture. "And we'll keep an extra eye on them for you."

"Thanks," Dr. Skylar replied. "I appreciate that. So, Ez and Luke, I see you got the Aquarius sweatshirts and the shorts we sent down. Please follow all the instructions you're given, and I want a full report when you surface in the morning." He leaned closer to the computer and whispered, "To tell you the truth, I'm a little jealous. Can only imagine what you'll see during the night."

Otter then pointed to a lipstick camera mounted on the ceiling. "There's no audio, but you'll be able to see what's going on throughout their overnight stay. This camera is on 24/7 in mission control."

Just then, a knocking sound drew everyone's

attention to the big viewport adjacent to the table.

Two divers in full-face masks hovered outside waving and indicating they were headed to the moon pool.

"Special delivery," noted Otter with a grin.

* * *

Becoming One with the Sea

After wrapping up the Zoom call, the team headed to the moon pool and watched as the two safety divers swam in. Lola lifted the transfer pot up to Otter before removing her full-face mask. "Did someone order... pizza?"

"No way," said Luke.

"Yes way," answered Lola as Otter removed the lid of the pot and took out two square slightly squashed cardboard boxes.

"Lucky there's not a lot of air in pizza," said Phil. "Though with the increased pressure down here, the crust gets a little compressed."

Gracie winked at Luke. "Excellent, if you're a thin crust lover like me."

"There she goes again," said her husband. "Always looking on the bright side."

From the transfer pot, Otter removed another package. It was round and covered in aluminum foil.

"Brought you a little surprise for dessert," announced Lola.

Zhao had removed his mask as well. "If you have any garbage or anything else to go up before decomp., we'll take it now."

Gracie went back into the main compartment of the station and returned quickly with a garbage bag. "Here you go." She turned to her husband. "Don't ever say I don't take out the trash." She then brought forward a hand that had been behind her back, revealing two cream-filled chocolate cookies. "And here's a tip for the delivery service."

Zhao grabbed a cookie. "Excellent."

Lola smiled and took the other. "Thanks, though kinda makes me feel like a trained dolphin getting treats as a reward."

"At least they didn't give us sardines," added Zhao, smiling as he chewed.

The others laughed and waved goodbye as the divers put on their full-face masks and headed to the surface. Ezzy watched, noting with relief that the water level in the moon pool was about the same as before.

Moments later, Drew popped up. He hung the long yellow hose and regulator on a hook. "Saw the divers. What'd we get?"

Luke grinned. "Pizza!"

Drew gave a thumbs up. "Hey Otter, I checked out those scratches on the forward viewport. No idea what could have done it. Don't look deep enough to cause a problem. But still odd."

"Roger that. We'll keep an eye on it. Let's go in and start prep for decomp."

Once inside the main compartment, Otter gathered everyone around the small table. "Okay, let me go over the safety protocols for our new aquanauts and then for decompression." He spent the next few minutes explaining what to do in case of emergencies and the procedure for decompression. "After the moon pool is sealed, the air pressure inside will be lowered over seventeen hours. By morning, the inside air will be at surface pressure. We'll then blow the pressure back down to equalize with the outside seawater pressure so we can get out and SCUBA dive to the surface."

"Now before we close and seal the moon pool," he continued. "If anyone has personal business to take care of, now is the time."

Ezzy cocked her head. "Huh? What kind of business?"

Luke snickered.

"What's so funny, smarty pants?"

Gracie gave Luke a mischievous smirk before turning to Ezzy. "He means if we have to go to the bathroom, we should go out now."

Ezzy's eyebrows shot up. "Whaaaat? Outside? But there's like a toilet inside."

"Yes, Ez," said Phil. "There is a toilet inside. But and that's a pretty big butt..." He winked at Luke who snickered again. "It gets backed up and that's not good in this confined environment. *So*, the preferred method is... to do it with the fish. Become one with the sea."

"You mean you want us to go to the bathroom out in the water?" Ezzy asked incredulously.

"It's actually very easy," Gracie told her. "Using the hose and regulator Drew just hung up, you put on your mask and then swim out to the gazebo, that white shed-like thing attached to the lab. It's half filled with high-pressure air so you can pop up inside to communicate and well, it's a good place to do your business. Best to do it when no other divers are around."

"Eeuw," moaned Ezzy.

"Actually, it's quite freeing," said Phil. "Except for one little problem."

"What's that?" asked Ezzy, not sure she wanted to know.

With a sheepish grin, Phil replied, "As it turns out, human waste is yummy fish food."

Ezzy groaned, "Even more eeuw."

"Some of the fish can be a little aggressive," added

Otter. "So just keep an eye out. But during decompression, if you need to go, the toilet is fine."

Ezzy decided she was going to hold it for as long as humanly possible, preferably until they were back on dry land.

"Personally, I prefer the inside option," noted Professor Miller. "Besides, I've always wondered about the nutrient load in the water around the lab."

"Oh, don't worry about that," said Otter. "We've actually taken measurements and the nutrients aren't any higher around the habitat."

"And it's why the fish are so fat and happy," Phil joked.

Luke laughed as Ezzy shook her head. "That's just *so* gross."

Gracie whispered to her, "It is a little, but you get used to it."

Those who wanted to "do their business" outside before decompression took turns going out. Luke decided to give it a try. Ezzy stood firm in her commitment to wait until they were back on dry land. After Luke returned from his visit to the gazebo, he began to describe what it was like to become one with the sea. Ezzy quickly held up her hand. "Stop right there, mister. No. I *do not* want to hear about your floating brown trouts."

The others laughed.

Otter and Drew began preparing the station for

decompression. Meanwhile, Professor Miller huddled by her computer watching as data streamed in from instruments on the reef. Gracie sat with Ezzy and Luke.

Phil approached the scientist. "Still seeing unusual conditions out there?"

"Spikes in the data seem to be coming in pulses, starting in the deep reef and then moving shallower."

"Do you think that's what caused the algae bloom?" Phil asked.

The scientist shrugged. "We get periodic upwellings or meanders from the Gulf Stream here, which could cause it. I suppose. But usually, the turbidity levels increase at the same time." She turned to Luke. "That's how much sediment, algae or stuff is in the water. It reduces the visibility. Here the oxygen and temperature both decreased but there was no change in the turbidity. I'm plotting the results on a map to see if there are any specific patterns."

A little bit later, after a quick call to mission control, Otter gave the thumbs up to the camera. "Okay everyone, here are the plans. We're ready to go. The moon pool is sealed tight, and the shore base crew is ready. For the first hour, as they start lowering the pressure from controls onshore, we're going to relax and breathe oxygen to start flushing the nitrogen from our bodies. Luke and Ezzy, you get to share the top right bunk. Phil and Gracie are in the middle bunks and Professor Miller is in the other top bunk. Drew and I are in the bottom two."

Otter and Drew distributed small masks connected by hoses to an oxygen canister.

"Just relax and breathe normal," Otter told them. "If you start feeling funny or unwell, let us know." He and Drew lay down and put masks on as well.

Ezzy lay still next to her brother. But Luke was fidgety. Ezzy elbowed him and he looked at her questioningly. "Stay still," she whispered through her mask.

Luke shrugged and had that scrunched up look on his face like he was deep in thought.

Ezzy wondered if he was nervous. Probably not, she decided. Apart from motion sickness, Luke was the ready-to-go-adventure kid, especially when it had anything to do with animals. She was the one who could be plagued by self-doubt, got nervous thinking too much, and had a wild animal phobia, which she hoped she was getting over. Ezzy inhaled and closed her eyes. She remembered in training that decompression sickness was called the bends because bubbles in the blood got trapped in joints, causing people to bend over in pain. She concentrated on her body. Her knee kind of hurt. *Was that the bends?* Then she remembered she'd bumped it on the ladder on the way up from the moon pool. Ezzy lay quietly, but she couldn't stop thinking about the bends. Was that a pain in her shoulder? Her big toe felt funny. Could there be a bubble in her blood trapped there? She felt a new pain in her arm, then realized it was Luke's elbow poking into her. She scooted away.

Over the next hour they went on and off breathing

pure oxygen. At one point, Ezzy heard a funny noise. She leaned over the bunk to look below. Phil had fallen asleep and was snoring through his oxygen mask. Ezzy snickered quietly.

"That's it for the oxygen," said Otter as he and Drew gathered everyone's masks. "Time for dinner and a little undersea entertainment."

*   *   *

Showtime After Dark

E zzy hopped down from the bunk, relieved that all her joints seemed to be working and bubble free—so far. She turned to the nearby viewport. It was dark. Nighttime had come to the ocean outside. She leaned closer. But with the lights on inside, all she could see was her own reflection on the big acrylic window.

"Who's ready for some pizza?" Gracie asked.

"Me!" Luke's hand shot up so fast, he nearly fell climbing down from the bunk.

"Me too," added Ezzy.

"Me three," said Phil.

They gathered around the table beside the viewport in the main compartment, squeezing onto the bench seats or standing nearby. Drew passed around the pizza boxes. "One's veggie, the other pepperoni. Sorry, it's cold. But we can't have a stove or oven down here." He made hand gestures to Ezzy and Luke suggesting a big explosion. "Have the microwave if you like hot but *soggy* pizza."

Minutes later, biting into a piece, Ezzy caught sight of Luke. He was chewing with a curious expression on his face. He turned to Otter. "Tastes kinda weird."

Ezzy chewed slowly. "Yeah. I can hardly taste my favorite part... the cheese."

Luke pumped his head up and down in agreement.

Phil chuckled. "Guess we should have warned you about the land of bland."

"The land of bland?" questioned Ezzy.

"Down here, your taste buds don't work the same as up top."

"Really?" said Luke. "How come?"

"We think it's the high pressure," responded Otter. "All that water on top of us. Down here everything tastes bland. Astronauts have a similar problem in space."

Ezzy took another bite and chewed thoughtfully. "It's not terrible, I guess."

"No worries. I have the solution," said Otter pulling a box from the shelving overhead. "Our excellent selection of hot sauces to spice things up." From the box he removed several small bottles and placed them on the table.

Ezzy grabbed one and read the label. "Mean green, kick-your-butt hot sauce."

Luke picked up another. "Sir fart-a-lot hot sauce." He laughed.

Ezzy noticed another bottle that had no writing, just a skull and crossbones on it. "I think I'll pass."

"Me too," said Luke.

"Wise move," whispered Gracie.

Otter winked and put a few drops of the skull and crossbones sauce onto his slice of pizza. Moments later he licked his lips. "Whooee, that's good."

Ezzy noticed a bead of sweat on the man's forehead as he reached for a glass of water.

After they'd polished off the pizza, Phil took the dish covered with aluminum foil out of the small refrigerator. "And now for dessert."

"What is it?" asked Gracie. "I have to admit to having a bit of a sweet tooth."

"You don't need any added sugar," gushed Phil. "You're already plenty sweet."

"Ugh," groaned Otter.

With a flourish, Phil whipped off the aluminum foil.

Professor Miller stared curiously at what was revealed. "What was it, might be the appropriate question."

It's definitely a pie, Ezzy thought. The crust around the outside looked pretty normal, but the topping looked like—white slime.

"I believe it's a lemon meringue pie," Otter told them. "At least that's what they said up top. Drew's lovely wife, Mattie, made it as a special treat."

Drew gave a weak thumbs up. Ezzy thought he looked more skeptical than enthusiastic. Maybe his wife wasn't a very good cook.

Gracie pulled a knife from a drawer. "I'll do the honors." She turned to her husband. "If you get the forks and plates, honey pie."

"Okay, lemon pie."

Ezzy chuckled as the others shook their heads good naturedly.

Gracie served each of them a slice of pie. Ezzy peered at hers with caution but decided to give it a try. As she put a forkful in her mouth, she noticed the look on Luke's face. This time it was obvious what he was thinking.

"Blech!" groaned Luke. "It... it tastes like goop."

Ezzy squinched up her face. "Make that no-flavor yellow goop."

"I've renamed it," Phil said with a smirk. "Under-the-sea-white-slime-yellow-goo-pie. No offense to your wife, Drew."

"None taken," Drew responded, placing his fork on the table, and pushing aside his piece of pie.

"At least we still have the regularly scheduled nighttime entertainment," said Otter.

"Entertainment?" asked Luke.

"Regularly scheduled?" said Ezzy.

Otter pointed to the big viewport at the front of the station in the bunkroom. "You two get the best seats in the house. We're gonna turn off the lights inside and turn on a few outside. And then... let the show begin!"

Ezzy had no idea what to expect as she and Luke went into the bunkroom and sat on the ends of the two lower bunks adjacent to the viewport. Phil and Gracie stood behind them in the aisle while Professor Miller sat at the table and peered out the slightly smaller side viewport in the main compartment.

"Ready?" Phil asked Luke and Ezzy.

"I was born ready," Luke replied.

"Oh brother," said Ezzy, rolling her eyes.

Otter smiled and flicked a couple of switches. Inside it went dark, while outside a spotlight shot through the water, shining down from atop the station. Ezzy and Luke watched curiously. Seconds later, tiny specks began to flit back and forth within the yellowy beam of light.

"What are they?" asked Luke.

"Zooplankton," answered Professor Miller from the other compartment. "Small animals. Many are copepods, little crustaceans. They're attracted to the light."

The group sat in silence watching as more tiny creatures began darting about amid the light. Some now wiggled like little worms. Others moved in miniature jumps. It was a swarm of wiggling darting living specks. A small silver fish then sped through the flickering mass. It was followed by another small fish zooming past.

"It's starting," announced Gracie.

"Right you are, sugar plum," noted Phil.

Ezzy stared as more fish darted by. One was larger with yellow stripes running lengthwise across its body. At the edge of the viewport, the tip of a red arm lined by white suckers slithered into view. Soon several bumpy red arms lined with small white suction cups attached to the acrylic. They crept across the viewport bringing with them a soft bumpy red body and a large bulbus head.

"It's an octopus!" announced Luke. "Awesome."

As if out for an undersea stroll, the octopus slithered slowly across the viewport. Ezzy leaned closer, marveling as the suckers latched onto and moved along the window. The octopus's entire body suddenly flashed fluorescent green. Then it was red again. At the far side of the viewport, the octopus stopped. It tilted its head and a horizontal eye slit opened as it peered in.

"What's it doing?" asked Ezzy.

"Octopus, like many creatures on the reef are nocturnal," said Gracie. "Meaning they are more active at night. This guy—or gal—comes by every night when we turn on the lights."

"I read that they're really smart and can change color super-fast," added Luke.

"Right you are," remarked Professor Miller. "They're also curious, strong, and can fit through amazingly small spaces."

"The ocean's own Houdini," added Otter.

The octopus detached its arms and slid away, out of sight. It was now all-out action in the illuminated water. Zooplankton flitted about as small fish darted in and out of the light. In a flash of silver, something bigger zoomed past. Then, gliding into view, came a silky white tube-like creature fronted by a ring of long skinny arms. It was about a foot long.

"That's a squid!" said Luke as it lunged forward and grabbed a fish before jetting away.

"It's the food web. in action," explained Professor Miller. "The light attracts the zooplankton, which attract the fish, which attract bigger predators, like the squid."

"Bigger predators?" said Ezzy. "Just how big are we talkin'?"

An even larger silver fish cruised into view. It had a pointy snout, razor sharp teeth, and a long narrow body with faint black stripes down its back. In its mouth hung the squid still holding the fish it had captured moments earlier.

"Whoa!" said Luke.

"Double whoa!" said Gracie. "Now that's not something you see every day."

"That's a barracuda," said Ezzy.

"So cool," said Luke. "How about sharks? Do you ever see them?"

"Sometimes," said Otter from the other compartment. "Most common out here are nurse or lemon sharks, sometimes hammerheads."

"That's okay, this is plenty," said Ezzy. Sharks were *definitely not* on her must-see list.

Luke turned to Ezzy. "A shark would be cool, sis."

Ezzy shook her head in response.

The group sat watching as the eat-a-thon continued. Fish darted in to eat the zooplankton. A few more squid cruised in for a snack and several fast silver fish with blue racing stripes entered the undersea buffet.

Otter leaned into the bunkroom. "Okay, everyone. Great show tonight, but we've got a long day ahead of us tomorrow and I'm sure everyone's pretty beat. About ten more minutes until curtain time."

Phil and Gracie Smith returned to the main compartment, but Ezzy and Luke stayed glued to the viewport.

"This is awesome," said Luke.

"Yeah," replied Ezzy. "Especially because we're in here, and the feeding frenzy is out there."

Luke chuckled. "Sis, people are not good fish food."

"*That* is exactly what I keep telling myself."

As if to end the show another large barracuda swam slowly into view with a squid sticking out of its mouth.

Luke shook his head. "Not very good table manners. Guess that guy's not worried about anything bigger eating it."

Ezzy was about to agree but stopped before the words came out. A humongous fish had cruised slowly into view behind the barracuda. She couldn't see its whole body, but it looked even bigger than Gertrude and Gandolf, the goliath groupers. It had long, waving frilly spines and glowing stripes. As Ezzy and Luke watched, it stealthily approached the barracuda and hovered unmoving behind the other fish. The barracuda seemed unaware of its presence. Then, without warning, the huge fish lunged forward open-mouthed and sucked in the barracuda, squid and all. Now bloated, the enormous fish slowly turned to face the viewport.

"OMG!" shouted Luke.

"Whaaaat is that?" added Ezzy.

"What is what?" asked Gracie from the main compartment.

The lights inside came on. Ezzy blinked in the brightness. When she looked at the viewport, again all she saw was her own reflection. "There's this really big fish out there. It ate the barracuda."

"And the squid. It was *really really* big," added Luke. "And glowing."

"A shark?" Gracie asked.

"I don't think so," answered Luke. "Can we turn on the outside light again?"

Otter turned off the inside lights and turned on the outside spotlights. A few fish flitted by. Ezzy stared intently. The giant fish was gone.

"Ahh guys," said Professor Miller pointing out the side viewport.

The others joined her in the main compartment. Ezzy slid onto the bench, next to the scientist. She leaned closer to the side viewport. At edge of the spotlight's illumination was a giant fish. Across its flank ran glowing stripes. Along its back and around its pectoral fins were huge waving frilly spines.

"What is it?" Ezzy muttered.

"Gertrude or Gandolf?" offered Luke.

"No," muttered Otter. "It looks like a lionfish."

The fish swam slowly out of view.

Drew shook his head. "But lionfish don't glow at night. And they definitely don't get that big."

*   *   *

Something Fishy

E zzy and Luke stayed glued to the viewport in case the strange and shockingly large fish returned.

"Maybe it's a new species of lionfish?" Professor Miller suggested.

Otter raised his eyebrows skeptically. "That big? And no one's ever seen it? If the hatch wasn't shut for decompression we could go out and get a photo."

"Could it have come up from deep water?" asked Luke.

That kid is brilliant, Ezzy thought. Why didn't she think of that? She'd heard that there are a lot of things we haven't discovered or seen in the deep ocean. Then again, Ezzy hadn't been thinking about where the fish came from, she was more worried about where it was going. As in where would it be in the morning when they headed to the surface? "If it is a lionfish, does that mean its spines are toxic like the smaller ones?"

"I really don't think it's a lionfish," responded Otter. "As for coming up from deeper water, probably not. It doesn't get deep here for quite a way offshore."

"Then what was it?" Phil asked. "And *where* did it come from?"

Otter shook his head. "I'll report it to mission control. Someone there might know something. In the meantime, why don't the rest of you get ready for bed. We've got a big day ahead of us tomorrow."

"I'm going to stay up a bit to work on the incoming data," Professor Miller said. "What's the word on that storm in the Caribbean?"

"Let's take a look," answered Drew as he pulled up a satellite image on a monitor nearby. A circular patch of red surrounded by yellow appeared southwest of Puerto Rico. "It's still a small storm moving west northwest. The track takes it over Cuba, where interaction with land could weaken it. Unfortunately, it's a waiting game to see what happens next. Plus, the water north of Cuba is very warm. If the storm weakens over Cuba, it could still rapidly intensify once it goes over all that warm water." He turned to Ezzy and Luke, smiling. "I actually majored in meteorology in school."

"Cool," said Luke.

Reaching into a storage bin in the overhead shelving, Gracie pulled out two toothbrushes and handed them to Ezzy and Luke. "They keep some spares down here. Even when you're living with the fish, clean teeth are important."

"Right you are, sugar plum," said her husband. "Besides, bad breath down here could be hazardous to all our health."

"There's toothpaste on the shelf above the sink in the other compartment," Gracie added. "And we just sleep in our clothes because they keep it pretty cold down here, so things stay dry."

Ezzy decided it was weird brushing her teeth fifty feet underwater while looking out the small viewport over the sink. She couldn't see much in the dark, but still it was strange. By the time she got to the bunkroom, Luke had already climbed up into their assigned top bunk. Ezzy scrambled up and squeezed in next to him.

"Nighty night," whispered Gracie as she climbed into her middle bunk. "See you in the morning."

"Don't let the undersea bed bugs bite," added Phil as he got into the one below them.

"Bed bugs?" Ezzy questioned.

"No," said Otter from the main compartment. "We *do not* have bed bugs down here. Lights out in a few minutes."

Luke chuckled and whispered to Ezzy, "Dad would

probably have said sleep tight, don't let the bed crabs bite."

"Or sleep tight don't let the bed snails bite," Ezzy responded, smiling.

"Wish he was here," Luke told her.

"Me too," Ezzy said. "I bet he wishes he was here too."

Luke shrugged sadly. "Mom would have loved it down here."

Ezzy nodded. "Yeah. By morning she probably would have devised some amazing plan to capture and identify that big creepy fish."

With a hint of a smile, Luke added, "You are so right."

The lights inside went out and Luke turned away from Ezzy, closing his eyes. "Night, sis."

As her brother drifted off, Ezzy lay still, thinking. She still missed her mom. It had gotten a little easier over time. But she still felt sad when she thought of her and when she wanted to share things or ask her questions. Ezzy's fingers naturally moved to her throat where she often wore one of her mother's scarves. She'd brought a couple to Florida, but none had made it into the undersea lab. She didn't wear a scarf every day anymore, and some had gotten pretty ratty. Her father had also started buying her new ones to add to her collection.

Ezzy then did a mental check for aches and pains, once again contemplating what bubbles in her blood might feel like. Again, so far, so good. No obvious signs of the bends. She heard someone climb into a lower bunk and figured it was either Drew or Otter.

Closing her eyes, Ezzy suddenly realized that while it was quiet inside the station, it was surprisingly noisy outside. There were all sorts of small pops, clicks, crackling, and loud snapping sounds. It was like a combination of popcorn popping and the sizzle of frying bacon. Ezzy leaned over the edge of the bunk to see if anyone else had noticed. But the others in the bunkroom were either asleep or nearly so. She turned toward the main compartment. Her view was now blocked by a curtain hanging down in the bunkroom entrance. Dim light filtered in around its edges.

Ezzy climbed quietly down from the bunk, taking care not to step on anyone below. She slipped through the curtain. Professor Miller was still at her computer, and Otter sat at the communications station looking at a variety of digital readouts and the satellite image of the storm. He turned as Ezzy entered the compartment. "Everything okay?"

Ezzy nodded. "I thought it would be quiet at night, but there's a racket going on out there."

Otter chuckled. "You get used to it after a while, but at first it seems pretty darn loud."

"What's making all that noise?"

"You mean all the click and clacks, and snapping?"

"Uh huh."

"Snapping shrimp on the reef are probably the

loudest. There's also fish and crabs feeding, and other creatures scuttling about. I think the metal of the station makes it all sound louder."

Otter moved over to the table near the viewport and indicated Ezzy should join him. With the lights dimmed inside, Ezzy thought she could make out some movement outside. "Do you think that big fish is still around?"

"Nah," answered Otter. "It's probably a nocturnal hunter. Now out on the reef looking for a good meal."

"Do you think it'll be out there in the morning?"

Otter smiled warmly. "I doubt it. Probably finds a place to hide during the day, otherwise we'd have seen it before. You know Ezzy, there are very few things out there that can hurt you. Especially if you go by some simple rules. Like don't touch or harass anything."

"What about sharks?"

"Actually, shark bites are almost always a case of mistaken identity. Sometimes it's murky and a shark mistakes a person for a fish or in some places a seal. Or if someone is spearfishing and carrying their fish. Can't really blame the shark there. People are truly not good shark food. Problem is, sharks taste by biting, so they don't know what they've bitten until it's too late. Don't get me wrong, sometimes sharks and people don't mix, and it can be tragic. But I've been diving in these waters for years and sure, I've been stuck by sea urchin spines, gotten stung by fire coral or those dang fire worms, but I've never had any bad encounters with sharks. Usually when they see you, they go the other way."

Ezzy desperately wanted to believe him. "You really think that big fish is gone and is nothing to worry about?"

Just as Otter was about to answer, they heard a high-pitched scraping noise like someone dragging their fingernails across a blackboard. Otter's brow furrowed as Ezzy winced.

"Whaat is that?" she asked as the noise continued. It seemed to be coming from underneath the lab.

Drew, Phil, and Gracie crept into the main compartment as the strange, screeching, wince-worthy noise continued. Then it abruptly stopped.

Phil looked around before whispering, "That's a new one."

"And not a very pleasant sound, I might add," said Gracie.

"Did you see anything outside?" Drew asked.

Otter shook his head. "Let's turn on the spotlights."

Drew nodded and flicked a switch. The spotlights over the two big viewports flashed on.

Ezzy put her nose up against the acrylic. A school of snappers rushed past and then an octopus jetted by. Following it was a big green moray eel racing away. "What's going on?"

"I don't know," answered Otter as he quietly slipped

through the curtain on his way into the bunkroom toward the big viewport at the front of the station.

Ezzy and the others followed as quietly as possible. They caught up to Otter who was crouched down in front of the viewport staring wide-eyed with his mouth agape.

"I think I know why all those creatures were in such a hurry to get away," Otter whispered pointing to the viewport. Looking in were three giant glowing fish with long frilly spines. Several more of the strange and enormous fish were swimming behind the ones staring at the viewport.

From Luke's bunk came a sleepy voice. "Hey, what's going on?"

"I think we found more of those really big creepy fish," whispered Ezzy.

"Or they found us," added Phil.

"Whoa!" said Luke as he nearly fell out of his bunk.

"Drew," Otter called out. "Turn the lights off. We don't want to create a buffet for these guys. Which is what we may have been doing each night by turning on the outside lights."

Drew flicked the switch, and the spotlights went dark. The fish remained visible, lit by their glowing stripes. There were six of them hovering together.

"It's like a pack of wolves," said Phil.

"Make that a school of big undersea swimming

wolves with long toxic spines," said Professor Miller from the main compartment. "I got an email from a fisheries biologist I contacted with a description of what we saw. He's never heard of or seen a fish like we described. He said to send a photo."

"Can't use a flash or we'll just get the reflection," said Otter. "We can try with the spotlight on, but the photo won't be very good."

One of the large fish turned and its long stiff spines scrapped along the viewport. The sound echoed inside the station, making everyone cringe.

"Well, I think I know where the strange marks on the viewport came from," announced Drew. "Otter, have your phone ready. I'm gonna turn the outside spotlight back on. See if you can get a photo."

Drew hit the switch and a yellow beam illuminated the big fish hovering by the viewport. Otter snapped a photo with his phone just as they swam away.

"Did you get one?" asked Luke.

"Not a *great* shot," replied Otter. "But I think I got enough of a photo of one for somebody to identify it. I hope. I'll send it to the folks onshore."

Drew turned the spotlight off. Otter sent the photo and then encouraged the others to go back to bed. Ezzy climbed into her bunk. Forget about the algae bloom, she thought, she was way more worried about the big creepy fish and where they would be in the morning when they SCUBA dived to the surface. A new thing-that-could-go-wrong-underwater just went to the top of her list—monster fish with huge spines filled with toxin. Ezzy tried to relax and not think about it. She lay awake for what seemed like hours before falling asleep.

* * *

Going Up!

E zzy woke with a start and, forgetting where she was, sat up. Clunk!

"Ow," she groaned softly, rubbing her head where it hit the low metal ceiling above the bunk.

Luke rolled over and sat up too. Clunk! "Ouch."

Ezzy turned to him, again rubbing her head. "Did the same thing."

The two teens scooted around to hang over the edge of the bunk.

Ezzy peered out the viewport. It was light out. "No creepy giant fish."

Luke scanned the other bunks. "Looks like everyone else is up already."

Gracie strolled through the curtain at the bunkroom entrance. "Our young aquanauts are finally awake. You two were so out, didn't even hear my handsome husband hit his head on the bunk overhead and fall out earlier."

A voice rang out from the other compartment. "Don't remind me. I'm not sure which hurts more, my head or my bottom area."

Ezzy tried not to laugh, but Gracie was rubbing her bum and making funny faces at them.

"Have you seen any more big, weird fish?" Luke asked. "Or sharks?"

"Nothing unusual so far," Gracie answered. "But we've got some nice, dehydrated eggs for you for breakfast."

Phil popped in, shook his head and stuck out his tongue. "I'd recommend my morning go-to meal... peanut butter and jelly sandwiches instead. Those just-add-water eggs are right up there with under-the-sea-white-slime-yellow-goo pie."

Luke raised his hand. "PB and J for me."

"Make that two," added Ezzy.

With her teeth brushed and face washed, Ezzy joined the others at the table in the main compartment. Outside the viewport, the sun's early morning rays pierced through the light blue water surrounding the station. On a nearby patch reef, small fish darted in and out of the coral. A few parrotfish swam by, heading below the undersea lab. It seemed very peaceful to Ezzy, especially compared to the previous night.

"Morning," said Otter as he walked in from the wet porch. "How are our junior aquanauts doing today? Ready to return to land-lubberville?"

Ezzy and Luke nodded as they chewed.

"Your dad called and is watching," Otter told them. "Wave at the camera."

They waved and held up their breakfast smiling.

"Okay then," said Drew. "Once you're finished, we'll get ready to blow this joint."

"Right," added Otter. "When the folks at mission control blow us back down to the same pressure as outside, remember we are at surface pressure now, we need to be ready to go. We'll have only about an hour to get to the surface after that or we'll need to go through additional decompression."

"What about the fish?" asked Luke. "The photo you sent?"

"No one has seen anything like it," answered Otter. "But everyone agrees, it looks like some very large species of lionfish. And by the way, folks up top report the algae bloom has moved toward shore. Should be safe to go up on regular gear."

Ezzy was so concerned about the big, creepy fish, she'd forgotten all about the green goopy water. It was a relief they wouldn't have to swim through it.

"And in case you were wondering about the storm," offered Drew. "I've just been reading the discussion from the experts at the National Hurricane Center. It's currently over Cuba and weakening, but it's still too early to tell what will happen when it moves off land and over the warm water north of the island. Forecast suggests there's little wind shear to break it up, so it has a good chance of strengthening."

Ezzy said silently to herself, *algae bloom gone, storm a maybe, no joint pains, and big creepy fish... hopefully somewhere else.*

"Okay everyone," announced Otter. "You each get a garbage bag for your stuff. The divers will bring everything up after we surface. And remember, there's no undersea maid service around here."

Ezzy and Luke got their bathing suits from the wet porch, changed, and packed their clothes and toothbrushes as souvenirs into a bag. They then helped the others pack gear, clean up, and prepare to leave.

"Do you want to take a package of dehydrated food to show your dad or friends at home?" Gracie asked.

"Sure," said Luke as he and Ezzy each chose a sample to put in their bag. Luke took a package of just-add-water blueberry cobbler, while Ezzy chose spaghetti and meatballs.

About twenty minutes later, Otter called mission control and gave them the go-ahead. "As they blow the pressure down, you may feel it in your ears much like diving. Squeeze your nose and blow out to release the pressure."

Ezzy sat with Luke at the table and waited, not sure what to expect.

"Here we go," said Otter. "Once the pressure is equal to outside, we'll open the moon pool so we can make our dive back to the surface."

A few minutes later, Ezzy felt pressure inside her ears as if she was descending on SCUBA. She turned to Luke nodding as she squeezed her nose and blew out. The pressure in her ears released. Over the next ten minutes or so she repeatedly cleared her ears as the pressure increased inside the undersea lab.

"That's it," announced Otter. "We're set to go. Everyone feeling okay?"

It was thumbs up all around.

Otter and Drew headed through the hydraulic door into the wet porch.

Ezzy peered out the viewport. "No giant lionfish in sight," she told the group before muttering, "At least that I can see."

A few minutes later Otter returned. "Drew's out by the moon pool and will help you get geared up. Divers from the surface will come down and accompany us up in pairs. Ezzy and Luke, you're up first."

Gracie stepped over to the table. "You two feeling good?"

"Fine," responded Ezzy.

"Good to go," answered Luke.

Sitting by her computer, Professor Miller glanced

toward them. "Watching the last bits of data stream in before calling it quits. Nice meeting you."

"Come on," said Gracie. "Phil and I will go with you out to the moon pool."

Otter was on the phone but nodded toward them. "Be out in a minute."

Ezzy took one last look around, trying to cement in her mind everything about the lab so she could tell her father all about sleeping with the fishes. She then followed Luke into the wet porch. Drew was standing by the moon pool, which was once again an open hatchway to the sea some fifty feet below the surface.

"Just waiting for the safety divers to pop down," noted Drew. "You two squeeze into your wetsuits and I'll grab your masks and fins."

Ezzy helped Luke pull on his wetsuit before she got into hers. It was damp and cold. She shivered, ready for some Florida sunshine. As Ezzy made her way to the moon pool, Otter burst through the hydraulic door.

"Hold on," he said. "The divers are back at the surface. We've got a little problem."

"Is the algae bloom back?" asked Luke.

Drew shook his head and pointed to the moon pool. "I think I know what the issue is. Make that two, rather large issues."

Phil and Gracie joined Ezzy, Luke, Drew, and Otter at the moon pool. Swimming in the shallow entryway were two of the giant lionfish. Their bodies were so big their long dorsal spines stuck out of the water.

"Uh, is this the only way out?" asked Ezzy.

"There's the escape hatch for emergencies under the floor in the main compartment," answered Otter. "But the safety divers reported more of those mutant fish under the lab where it opens up."

Ezzy's heart began to race. "What do we do now?"

"Maybe we can scare them away," said Drew leaning down and splashing with a dive fin.

The two fish turned and darted forward as if to attack the fin.

"Yup, don't think that's gonna work," noted Phil.

"The safety divers are going to try to use spearguns to scare them away," said Otter. "Let's all stay ready to get in and make a swim for the surface. We do not want to get back into decompression time."

Phil and Gracie put on their wetsuits. Luke stayed glued to the moon pool watching the lionfish. Ezzy paced back and forth beside him. She did not want to get in the water with those fish. This time sharp teeth or claws weren't what concerned her. It was their long thick spines full of poison.

Some fifteen minutes later, a radio in the wet porch crackled. Otter picked it up. "We're ready when you are. Roger that." He hung the radio up on a hook. "The divers are on their way down."

The group gathered around the moon pool. The fish turned to face outward and made small but strong swishing movements with their fins. Ezzy thought they seemed agitated. One shot out the entryway. The other quickly followed.

"Yay," shouted Luke.

"We're not out of here yet," muttered Ezzy.

One of the safety divers popped up in the moon pool. It was Lola. She removed her regulator. "Okay guys, Zhao is standing guard keeping those fish away. But we need you to get in and head for the surface. Remember you still need to go slow and exhale to be safe."

Ezzy turned to Otter. "You still want us to go first?"

"Yes," he replied. "Phil and Gracie, you two get ready to follow on their heels. We're not going to wait for the divers to come back. I'll go with you, and Drew will accompany the professor after that."

"You can do this," Gracie said to Ezzy. "Just remember your training. Don't go up any faster than the bubbles around you and keep breathing regularly."

"That's not what I'm worried about," Ezzy said.

"We'll keep the fish away," Lola assured her.

Luke scampered down the ladder into the moon pool next to Lola. Drew handed him his mask and fins. Ezzy climbed down next.

"Lola will help you put on your tanks," said Drew. "I filled them so you've got more than enough air for this short dive and the same weights are in the pockets as before so you should be neutrally buoyant."

Luke nodded. Ezzy tried to smile but couldn't muster it. She swiveled her head, looking around the moon pool for the fish. She saw Zhao's fins as he lay on the metal grating floor guarding the entrance.

Lola helped them put on their buoyancy compensators and tanks. "Piece of cake," she told Ezzy and Luke.

"My dad would say piece of pumpkin pie," Luke said with a forced chuckle.

Ezzy was too nervous to add anything.

"Okay," said Lola. "Put your fins and masks on. Yup, that's good. Now regulators in your mouths. Take a test breath to be sure everything is working."

Ezzy breathed in. Air flowed freely into her mouth. She exhaled. She took another breath and tried to relax, silently repeating, I *am not good fish food. I am not good fish food.* Adding, *I can do this.*

"Go ahead and duck down and stay behind Zhao," Lola told them. "I'll be right behind you, watching your back."

Luke nodded and ducked under. Ezzy took a deep breath, tried to exhale slowly, and did the same. Zhao swam out from the undersea lab. Luke and Ezzy followed. They stayed side by side as they glided out from under the station. Ezzy immediately swiveled her head, looking around. Several of the giant lionfish were hovering below the undersea lab and seemed to be watching them. Ezzy wondered where the rest were. Zhao rose slowly. Ezzy and Luke followed.

Ezzy tried to stay calm and breathe normally. It wasn't easy. Her heart pounded and she felt like she wasn't getting enough air. Through his mask, Ezzy could see that Luke's eyes were wide, but still he seemed calm. He probably wasn't even thinking of all the ways they could die going up—poked by poison-filled spines, air embolism (she learned about those in SCUBA class), the bends, or sharks. Ezzy told herself she was thinking too much. She had to be more like Luke and just go with it. Besides, this was the new and improved Ezzy. She exhaled and slowly rose toward the surface.

They continued to rise amid their bubbles with Zhao now on one side and Lola on the other like undersea bodyguards. Ezzy checked the depth on her dive computer. Forty feet. Thirty-eight feet. Movement to the left drew her attention. Swimming toward them was one of the humongous lionfish. To the right, another huge lionfish appeared. Ezzy and Luke drew together while Lola and Zhao swam protectively at their sides. Ezzy looked down and saw Phil, Gracie, and Otter heading out of the undersea station. She swallowed hard and told herself to remain calm.

The lionfish swam closer. Zhao poked at one with a spear, and it veered off. Lola held her spear out threateningly, but the other fish seemed undaunted. It dove and swam in between the two groups of divers. Lola followed it, keeping it away from them.

Out of the blue swam another lionfish, its toxic spines fluttering menacingly. It headed straight for Luke. Without thinking, Ezzy pulled him closer and scooted in front of him. The lionfish swam closer. Soon she was face to face with the giant poison-spined fish. Ezzy closed her eyes and waited to get stuck.

Suddenly, a loud deep thump echoed through the water. Around Ezzy, the sea seemed to convulse. She opened her eyes.

Swimming around the group of divers were two more giant fish. But they weren't the enormous lionfish. It was Gertrude and Gandolf. The goliath groupers. As the groupers circled, they rapidly opened and closed their mouths creating a series of booming thumps. Ezzy spun around. The sound and concussions in the water had scared the lionfish away. Six of them now huddled together beneath the undersea lab.

Zhao and Lola led Ezzy and Luke up to the surface, where waiting hands hauled them rapidly up and into the boat. They removed their regulators as their father pulled them into a tight hug. "Thank god!"

"Gertrude and Gandolf saved us, Dad," gushed Luke.

"Gertrude and Gandolf?"

"Two goliath groupers," Ezzy explained. "They made these big booms with their mouths and scared away the lionfish."

"Wow!" said Dr. Skylar.

"It was amazing," exclaimed Luke.

Already out of her gear, Lola had come over to help Luke and Ezzy with their equipment. "Yahoo for

Gertrude and Gandolf. That booming is what they do when they're protecting their territory. In this case. I think they were also protecting us, thankfully."

Ezzy sat down on a bench along the side of the boat and breathed slowly, trying to get her heart to stop pounding. She watched as the other divers arrived at the surface and boarded. With relief, she noted Drew come aboard, figuring he was last out of the station just after Professor Miller, who had already climbed into the boat. Everyone had made it up safely.

Sitting across from Ezzy, Drew began to pull off his fins. "Uh guys," he said wincing. "I might have a little issue." He drew in a deep breath. "On the way out, one of those fish got a little too close. I kicked it and I think a spine got my ankle, between my fin and wetsuit." He held up a foot. Rivulets of bright red blood streamed down. It had begun to swell and turn an ugly shade of red.

"Dang it," said Otter as he grabbed a towel and threw it to Drew. "Always trying to be the hero."

Dr. Juan, the base doctor, was aboard the boat. He grabbed a first aid kit and ran to Drew's side. "Call 911 and have an ambulance waiting at the dock," he told the captain.

Drew lay back, clearly in pain. "That seems a bit excessive."

"Everyone reacts differently to these toxins," said Dr. Juan. "And this looks like a new species. We have no idea how you are going to respond. The fast rescue boat is already on its way out. I called them just in case as soon as I heard about the lionfish down there. I'm going to clean, disinfect and dress the wound, and then put some heat on it. Heat is the best treatment to begin to break down the toxin."

Ezzy and the others watched with growing concern.

"I'm a doctor as well," offered her father. "Let me know if there's anything I can do."

Dr. Juan took an instant heat pack from the first aid kit and applied it to the cleaned and bandaged wound. "We need to watch for shock and breathing difficulties."

About ten minutes later, Ezzy heard the roar of a powerboat approaching. She turned toward the sound. A large rooster tail of water fountained behind a boat racing toward them. It had big twin engines at the stern.

"Okay, Drew," said Dr. Juan. "We're going to transfer you to the other boat. Can you stand?"

Drew attempted to rise, but only made it to a sitting position. "Little woozy and not sure I can put any weight on my foot."

"Stay right there," said Otter. "We've got you."

As the approaching powerboat slowed, the dive team gathered around Drew. By the time the boat was alongside, he had been lifted off the deck. Dr. Juan supervised as the team gently passed him to the staff on the other boat. Grabbing his medical bag, Dr. Juan turned to Dr. Skylar. "I'm going to ride in with Drew, could you keep an eye on everyone else on the way in?"

"Of course."

Dr. Juan climbed into the other boat as Drew was settled on a bed of towels on the deck. The driver of the rescue boat pulled slowly away before pushing the throttles forward. The engines roared, and the boat rocketed toward shore.

"Okay, our turn to head in," said Otter. "Another team will be out to pick up the gear left below and close things up."

"What about the giant lionfish?" Luke asked.

"Maybe my pals Gertrude and Gandolf will scare them off and reclaim Aquarius as their own again. If not, we'll just have to avoid them or if necessary, might be lionfish for dinner."

Luke's eyes got wide. "I thought they were toxic?"

"Oh, that's just the spines," answered Otter. "The smaller ones are quite tasty. It's a flaky white fish. We even have Kevlar gloves to use while cutting off the spines. In fact, the local restaurants serve lionfish and encourage fishing. These might be a little trickier to get, but just one could provide a meal for the entire team."

"But if this is a new species," said Luke. "How do you know the meat isn't toxic too?"

Yup, that kid is brilliant, thought Ezzy.

Otter put his hand to his chin. "Hadn't really thought of that. Good point. Guess we'll need to get it tested."

"Maybe sharks will eat them," suggested Luke.

"Unlikely," responded Professor Miller. "They're not their natural prey. Have no history of eating them here."

Ezzy shook her head. "One thing for sure. I'm staying on dry land until those big creepy lionfish are caught."

"Catching them might be tricky," said Otter. "I think it's curtains for those invaders. And even that might not be so easy."

"Yeah," said Luke turning to his sister. "Imagine trying to capture one of those."

Ezzy wanted no part of that plan. "Well, I hope you guys or someone can capture or kill them. Either way is okay by me."

"I wonder where they came from?" asked Luke. "I mean how did they get here?"

Dr. Skylar tussled his son's hair. "That's another very good question."

*   *   *

Return to Land

E zzy, Luke, and the others arrived at the dock in Key Largo well after the ambulance had transported Drew to the hospital. Their boat was tied up behind the rescue vessel beside the sea station's headquarters, also known as mission control. As soon as the lines were secured, Ezzy leapt out and ran for the door, yelling back to her father, "Bathroom."

Luke giggled. "Guess she held it, all right."

Dr. Skylar shrugged. "When ya gotta go, ya gotta run."

Mission control was housed in a redesigned waterfront mini-mansion. Renovations had been made so that it now included a high-tech briefing room, a 24/7 monitoring station, several offices, a kitchen, storage areas, a workshop, and a small medical facility, including an emergency decompression chamber. The adjacent canal led to the ocean, and from there, it was about a four-mile boat ride to the undersea station. Next to the operations base was another home that had been transformed into a dive locker, small laboratory, and visitor suites.

After a brief check in with Dr. Juan, Ezzy and Luke took long hot showers in their assigned suite. Joining their father, they then headed next door where they found Otter and Professor Miller in the briefing room. Ezzy thought of it as a cool, cozy, high-tech classroom. The furniture consisted of mismatched couches, comfortable chairs, and small tables. On one wall hung a large flatscreen. Beneath it was a row of smaller screens. In the back, off to one side, was a kitchen, separated from the rest of the room by a long black countertop and stools.

"Any word on Drew?" Dr. Skylar asked. "How's he doing?"

Otter nodded. "He's resting but still in some pain. Should make a full recovery."

"Glad to hear it."

"What about the giant lionfish?" asked Luke. "Did they catch them?"

Otter shook his head. "When the team went back to get the gear, the lionfish were gone. Gertrude and

Gandolf were back under the station. No one has seen any of the giant lionfish since."

Sitting on a couch with a laptop computer on her knees, Professor Miller looked up. "They might be mostly nocturnal. Spending most days hidden somewhere until dark."

"Maybe that's why no one's ever seen them before," suggested Luke.

"Maybe," responded Otter.

Ezzy shrugged. "But how come they attacked us in the morning, then? They should have been hiding."

"Good question, Ez," said her father.

She smiled proudly.

Professor Miller cocked her head in thought. "Could be that they were trying to show their dominance at the habitat if they wanted it to become their territory. We might have been attracting them with the light show each night without even knowing it."

"Then how come they didn't come around before?" asked Luke.

"Not sure," answered the professor. "Maybe they had to get to be a certain size before they were ready to take over new territory."

"Do you think they're gone for good?" Ezzy asked.

"Hard to say."

Luke raised his hand. "What about the algae bloom?"

Otter stood and picked up a tablet from a table. "As a matter of fact, Professor Miller and I were just discussing that. She was about to show me what she's discovered."

He encouraged the Skylars, along with Gracie and Phil Smith, who had just walked in, to take a seat. Otter tapped the tablet. Curtains closed across the floor-to-ceiling windows and the sliding glass door overlooking the canal. He tapped again and the lights dimmed while the large flatscreen on the wall flickered on. "Is your computer connected to WiFi?" he asked the scientist.

"Good to go," she replied.

Ezzy watched curiously, noting the images on the row of smaller screens. One looked like the weather radar images her local meteorologist showed on television, except this one was of the Florida Keys. Another screen had a wider view radar image with the storm crossing Cuba along with a cone depicting the forecast track. The last screen displayed a view from inside the undersea lab.

An image came up on the large flatscreen. Ezzy recognized it as a view from above the ocean looking down on the reefs around the sea station. She could see the yellow outline of the undersea lab sitting in a horse-shoe shaped patch of sand surrounded by patches and ridges of brownish green mounds, which she assumed were coral reefs.

Ezzy noted how the ridge-like coral reefs ran perpendicular to shore, going from shallow to deep water. Between the ridges were grooves or chutes of sand.

For some reason it reminded her of the kids' game *Chutes and Ladders.* Where it got shallower, the reefs were more patchy. Ezzy then noticed a bunch of black lines superimposed over the reefs. Some ran parallel to shore and others were like the legs of a spider stretching out from the undersea research station. "What are the black lines?"

Otter stepped to the screen and pointed to the thin dashed lines running parallel to shore. "These show the bathymetry or depth. This line is at twenty feet and then down here at the base of the reefs is one showing 100 feet."

"What are the other lines?" Luke asked.

"That's our undersea highway system. They're cables suspended just above the reefs and run out from the lab."

"I know what those are for," offered Gracie, winking at Ezzy. "In case the aquanauts are out working on the reef and visibility goes ka-pooey. There are plastic arrows on the cables that divers can use to feel their way back to the station even if they can't see."

"Right you are, sugar plum," said Phil. "Before we started living in the station, we had to train, without masks, on how to use the cables to find our way back just in case."

"That's all well and good," said Professor Miller. "But here's the real interesting stuff." Clicking rang out as her fingers flew across her keyboard. A set of blinking red dots popped up on the image. "Those are my sensor locations. Make that were my sensor locations."

"Sorry," Otter told her. "But we had to pull them with the storm potentially approaching. Better to retrieve them now than have them either destroyed or washed away."

Professor Miller nodded reluctantly before navigating an arrow on the screen to one of the blinking red dots. She clicked on it. Lines of data and a graph popped up. "This station at ninety-five feet to the north of the undersea lab is where the anomalous conditions began."

"Anomalous conditions?" Ezzy asked.

"That's science-speak for strange or unexpected data," explained Phil.

"It's where the sensors first detected cold, low salinity, low oxygen water," said the scientist. She then pointed the arrow on the screen to several other red dots. "Later the sensors picked it up here to the south near the station and then here and here at the shallower stations toward shore."

"What does that tell you?" asked Dr. Skylar.

"Well," said the scientist. "Looks like whatever it is started in deep water, coming either from farther offshore or from the deeper reefs, and then flowed south and toward the surface."

"Is that what caused the algae bloom?" asked Luke.

"I'm not a scientist," said Otter. "But that's what I'd bet on."

"What was it?" Ezzy asked, wondering if someone did it on purpose and if there was any connection to the giant lionfish.

"That's the million-dollar question," noted Phil.

"I see two likely options," noted Professor Miller. "One, is water upwelling caused by a meander of the Gulf Stream. Which means as the current swung toward shore, it caused cold, nutrient-rich water to flow up over the reefs. But look at this." She clicked a few keys, and a new image came up on the screen. "This is a satellite image of sea surface temperature."

Ezzy stared at the image. It showed the land in black along the southeast coast of the US. A short distance to the east and offshore was a winding river of red that stretched from Florida north to about North Carolina. There, it appeared to curve to the right. Further to the north were some weird swirls with yellow centers and to the south, similar swirls with green centers.

"Is the red the Gulf Stream?" asked Luke.

"Very good," said Professor Miller.

Of course, Luke figured it out, Ezzy thought, once again proud and a little jealous of her quick thinking and remember-everything-he-reads brother.

"The red is the warmest water," said the scientist. "Followed by yellow then green and blue as it gets colder. Notice how it's all red to the south and into the Gulf of Mexico. That's where the warm water that makes up the Gulf Stream comes from. It flows from the Caribbean into the Gulf of Mexico where it sometimes loops around and then feeds the Gulf Stream."

"What are those swirly things up there?" Ezzy asked pointing to the strange circular looking patches.

"See how the Gulf Stream turns to the east off North Carolina?" asked the scientist.

"Uh huh."

"As the current flows, particularly in that area, big meanders or curves form that get cut off and it creates eddies or rings. That's what you call those swirly things. They're patches of circling water that have broken off the Gulf Stream. The ones to the north of the current with the yellow or red centers are warm core rings and to the south with the green centers are cold core rings."

"Cool," said Luke.

"Or warm," added his father.

Ezzy shook her head at her father.

"The eddies help to mix the ocean and can even transport sea creatures within them."

"Whoa," said Luke. "Could one of those be what brought that weird water onto the reefs?"

"Or the giant lionfish?" asked Ezzy.

"Probably not the fish," said Professor Miller. "But they could be a source for the water. But this image is from around the time of our mission. There are no strong meanders or eddies off South Florida. At least at the surface, that is. Unfortunately, satellite images only show the temperature at the sea surface, in the top few centimeters."

"If not a meander or one of those swirly things," said Phil. "What's option number two?"

Professor Miller switched back to the image of the area around the sea station. She positioned an arrow on the blinking red dot at ninety-five feet north of the station. "Could have something to do with the land that makes up the Florida Keys."

"Huh?" said Ezzy.

Gracie put her hand up. "Oooo, let me. I know. The Florida Keys are made of limestone and it's very porous. That means there are *lots* of holes in it." She then waved like a queen to the adoring masses.

Her husband pretended to bow to her in appreciation. "Your Highness."

Ezzy chuckled quietly.

"That's right," said Professor Miller. "Option number two is groundwater flowing under Key Largo and into the ocean at the deep reefs."

"But how would that cause the pea-soup water?" asked Ezzy.

"If it was *polluted* water," said Luke proudly.

"Ding. Ding," said the scientist. "Exactly. If the groundwater was high in nutrients due to runoff or wastewater being pumped into the ground, it could trigger a bloom when it reached the surface and sufficient sunlight."

"So, you think polluted water seeping out in the deep reefs caused the bloom?" Otter asked.

Professor Miller shook her head. "I'm not saying it caused it for sure. I'm *suggesting* that groundwater unusually high in nutrients coming out on the deep reefs *could* have caused it."

Otter turned on the lights and moved to a map hanging on another wall. "Here's a map of the land adjacent to the reefs." He pointed offshore. "This is Conch Reef where the station is located, and if we go a little north, this is about where Professor Miller's deep sensor was."

Otter ran his finger west several miles to shore. He tapped an area and said, "This is to the west of that sensor. Previous research has shown that groundwater moves from west to east in the underlying limestone."

"What's there?" asked Phil.

Otter leaned closer to the map. "There's some residential housing, a few restaurants, and a large resort complex with a big marina. Slightly to the west of that is a fish farm, but they use a closed system. Wastewater was a concern when it was being planned, but I know they're not releasing any wastewater or fish."

"My bet is on the resort then," said Phil. "I bet they're injecting their wastewater."

"Careful," said Professor Miller. "It could be runoff from roads and other stuff just seeping into the ground."

Ezzy's money was on Phil's theory. Evil scheme, bad intentions, negligence, or something like that.

"I think we should check out the resort," offered Phil.

Just then they heard a door open and a voice yell, "Dad?"

Otter smiled. "Looks like lunch is here, along with someone special. We can discuss this more after I've filled my belly and gotten a hug."

* * *

Flavor's Back

T he boy ran in with unbridled glee. He was thin, about Ezzy's height with a mop of unruly curly red hair and unusually pale skin. He leapt into Otter's arms and hugged the man as if he'd been away for months. Ezzy watched with a smile, soaking up the obvious warmth between Otter and the boy.

"Dad!"

"Alec!"

"I missed you."

"No, I missed you more."

Otter kissed his son and then blew a loud raspberry on his forehead. The boy giggled, stepping back.

"Hey everyone, this is my son Alec."

The others waved and smiled at the boy. He didn't return their gaze. Instead, he stared down as if contemplating the nature of his shoes. He wore black board shorts and a t-shirt several sizes too big. It was blue and decorated with fish as if they were swimming across the fabric.

"He can be a little shy," noted Otter.

"Hi Alec," said Gracie. "It's nice to meet you. How old are you?"

"How old are you?" Otter repeated.

Alec shook his head.

"He just turned twelve," Otter said.

Ezzy tried not to stare at the boy. She wondered if he was simply shy or if it was something else. In her class at school there was a kid with autism. In some ways, he reminded her of Luke after their mother died. The boy was shy and didn't talk a lot. Sometimes he got upset. Thinking of Luke, she'd made an effort to be friends with him. His name was Josh. When she told Josh about how her brother, Luke, loved animals, he started talking to her more, asking her about animals. She later introduced Josh to Luke, and they'd become friends. Two peas in a pod when it came to animals. She watched Alec repeatedly smooth out his shorts and run his fingers across the fish on his shirt.

Luke stepped forward. "Hi, I'm Luke. Cool shirt. Did you hear about the fish we saw?"

Alec's head snapped up. "Fish? What kind?"

"Really really big lionfish."

"Lionfish," Alec repeated. "I like fish."

Otter tussled the boy's hair. "He doesn't just like fish. Alec loves fish."

The boy nodded vigorously before again staring at his feet.

Another staff member who'd arrived with Alec set out platters of salads and sandwiches, along with a basket of potato chips. As soon as Ezzy saw the food, her belly rumbled. She fidgeted and glanced about to see if anyone had noticed the outrageously loud noises coming from her stomach.

Otter led his son to the countertop. "Dig in, everyone. It's not here for looks. Alec, how about a ham and cheese sandwich?"

Although the boy didn't respond, Otter placed a sandwich on a plate along with some chips. He then filled a plate for himself before leading his son to a couch where they sat down to eat.

Minutes later, with everyone's mouth full and chewing, the room became noticeably quiet. Ezzy sat happily next to Luke and her father munching on chips and a sandwich.

Phil smacked his lips loudly. "Mmm, the flavor is back!"

"Never has a grilled veggie sandwich tasted so good," added Gracie.

Luke nodded. "After the land of bland in the undersea lab, this sandwich tastes super good."

"You know what they say. A sandwich a day keeps the doctor away," said his father.

Luke shook his head. "*Dad!* That's a *really* bad one."

Ezzy nodded. "An *apple* a day keeps the doctor away."

"Now, as I was saying before we all got distracted by this excellent and thankfully good tasting food," said Phil. "I think we should check out that resort to see if they are contaminating the groundwater."

Otter looked up. "No can do today. You're all restricted to base for the next twelve hours. It's just a precaution in case there are any side effects from decompression."

"How about tomorrow then?" asked Phil as he pointed to the small screen showing the storm passing over Cuba. "We're sticking around for a few days, and it looks like we have a day or two before that storm arrives."

"Won't stop you if you want to check out the resort," responded Otter. "But *please* do not accuse them of anything or imply that we think they're contaminating the groundwater or reef. At least not without solid proof. This is a small community and things have a way of getting out and blowing up."

Alec's eyes got wide. "Blowing up?"

"It's just an expression," Otter told the boy. "Not really blowing up, more like making people upset."

Gracie smiled. "Oh, no worries. We are very good

at acting like we don't know anything. We'll simply be elderly travelers checking out the resort for our next visit."

"Can we go too?" Ezzy asked her father. She liked figuring things out with the Smiths and felt safe when they were around.

"Good idea," said Phil. "You and your brother could be on holiday helping your aging grandparents."

"Maybe not," responded Dr. Skylar. "I'd prefer you two don't get mixed up in any unofficial detective work by our sneaky friends here. We have a few days before leaving and I'm sure we can find something else to do."

Otter whispered to his son before saying, "Hey, I've got an idea. Alec works as an intern slash volunteer at that fish farm I mentioned. That's how I know they aren't dumping their wastes. He's going over there in the morning. He loves it." He gave his son a one-arm hug. "Maybe you could go with him. It's cutting-edge technology and pretty neat."

Dr. Skylar looked to his kids. "What do you think?"

"Sure," answered Luke. "Sounds cool."

"Sure, why not," agreed Ezzy. "What kind of fish do they raise?"

Otter turned to Alec. "What kind of fish are at the farm?"

"Almaco Jack, Pompano and *Nemo*," said Alec.

"They raise fish for eating," added Otter. "And have a program for ornamental fish."

"Ornamental fish?" asked Ezzy, thinking it sounded like something you'd put in your yard like a plastic flamingo.

"Fish for aquariums," said Otter.

"Okay, then it's all set," announced Gracie. "We'll be the doddering elderly couple checking out the resort and you all go see the fish."

"Right you are, my favorite granny," said Phil, kissing his wife. "Did we bring our canes?"

"You know it, grandpa."

Ezzy shook her head, smiling.

"For the rest of the day and for tonight," said Otter. "Please relax. Nothing too energetic. Rest. We'll put some food out for dinner around 6PM and show a movie on the big screen. We'll also be keeping an eye on the storm. Come by any time if you'd like additional information. It's currently over Cuba and seems to be weakening, which is good. But the team is still going out this afternoon to retrieve gear and do early preparations in case the storm strengthens. And of course, if you have any problems or don't feel well, text, call or swing by here or the medical room."

After lunch, the Skylars and Smiths said goodbye to Otter and his son, along with Professor Miller, and returned to the suites next door. The cell phone and internet connections were poor, so they spent the afternoon napping, watching television, and reading books.

Around 6 PM, the group returned to mission control for dinner and a movie. Otter had chosen one of his favorites, *The Abyss.*

After watching the movie, Ezzy was glad they hadn't seen it before visiting the undersea laboratory. In the movie a hurricane hits, a crane falls off a boat and nearly hits an underwater station, which is then dragged to a cliff. Someone living underwater purposely drowns and is resuscitated. And then there's a weird twist at the end in which aliens save the station and all the people. Luke and her father loved it. They thought the special effects were fantastic. Ezzy worried she'd have nightmares.

Later, as she lay in bed, Ezzy thought about the movie and then reflected on what it was really like in the undersea lab. She thought about how Gertrude and Gandolf had knocked her over and remembered what it was like to climb out of the moon pool into air fifty feet below the surface. How Phil had scared her with the creature-from-the-black-lagoon mask and how hard Luke had laughed. She thought about how the pizza tasted funny, about hearing all the snaps and crackles outside the lab at night, and what had happened when they turned on the spotlight. Then she thought about the big lionfish. Make that creepy, mean, big lionfish. She wondered if they had returned to the undersea lab that night and where they'd come from. Her eyelids began to feel heavy, and soon she drifted off to sleep.

*   *   *

The Fish Farm

A t base headquarters the next morning, the Skylars were enjoying breakfast when Phil and Gracie Smith shuffled in. Ezzy chuckled at their appearance. Dr. Skylar nearly spit out his orange juice. Gracie walked stooped over leaning heavily on a cane. The old-fashioned flowery print dress she wore reminded Ezzy of a flannel nightgown she once owned. Phil too had a cane, and was outfitted in high black socks with sneakers, long, ill-fitting shorts hiked up to his waist, and a tucked-in well-worn pink polo shirt.

Dr. Skylar shook his head. "Don't you think that might be overdoing it a bit?"

Gracie turned stiffly to face him. "What'd ya say, honey? Speak up."

"Wants to know if you want a muffin, Hon," stuttered Phil.

"A muffler," croaked Gracie. "Why would I want a muffler?"

Luke giggled. Ezzy grinned. Dr. Skylar stifled a laugh.

With dramatic flair, Phil threw away his cane and jumped into a superman pose. Gracie threw her cane onto a nearby couch and leapt into a similar stance. "So, what do you think? Are we good or what?"

"You'd fool me," Ezzy said.

"They already did," noted Luke. "In the Galápagos."

"This might be going a bit overboard," repeated Dr. Skylar.

"Nah," responded Phil. "People eat it up. It's all about expectations. Old age bias."

Dr. Skylar shrugged. "If you say so."

"We've already rented a car and plan to head over to that resort later this morning," said Phil. "Nothing we like better than a juicy investigation into potential wrongdoing."

Ezzy wished she was going along.

Phil turned to Dr. Skylar. "When are you guys going to the fish farm?"

"Otter should be by in about fifteen minutes."

"Maybe we'll be having fish for dinner," said Gracie winking at them. "I know Otter said they're not releasing their wastewater, but just in case, stay on the lookout. You never know."

Ezzy nodded with enthusiasm. "I'll keep an eye out."

*   *   *

Otter picked the Skylars up as promised and along with his son, Alec, they headed to the fish farm. As they were leaving, Ezzy caught a glimpse of the Smiths already back in character: stooped over, leaning heavily on their canes. Again, she wished she was going with them. But maybe she could still be part of the investigation by checking out the fish farm. Maybe Otter didn't know everything going on there.

Ezzy turned to Luke to tell him to stay on the lookout for anything suspicious at the fish farm. But given the gray pallor of his face and tendency to get car sick, she decided to tell him later.

It was a quick drive across the highway running the length of the Florida Keys and down a few backroads to the broken-shell-lined parking lot next to a sign reading: *Unhooked Fish Farm*. A white two-story building on stilts sat beside the parking area. Behind it were a series of long rectangular white buildings that reminded Ezzy of big tents set up for parties.

Otter parked the car. "The fish farm is on the Bay side of the Keys," he told them, pointing to a mangrove lined shore and open body of water to their left. He then led them up a stairway to the entrance of the building on stilts. "We'll check in and then I've got to head back to base to check on storm prep. Call when you're ready to leave."

Stepping inside the building, Ezzy silently thanked the inventor of air conditioning. Inside it was cool and dry compared to the summer furnace outside. She scanned the room they'd entered. A series of offices lay behind a counter where an older woman sat in front of a computer. The rest of the area was like a nature center. Scattered about were interactive displays, posters, and nature videos playing on big flatscreens.

"Hey, dude!" said a young man to Alec as he exited the office area. His skin was mocha colored, and his dark hair stuck out in shiny corkscrews that bounced rhythmically with his gait.

Ezzy considered her frizzy brown ponytail now hanging limply down her back and envied the young man's lustrous curls. She watched him with interest, noting his warm smile and confident swagger. He stepped up to Alec raising a fist. Alec grinned and fist bumped him.

Otter shook his head good naturedly. "Here we go."

The two boys clapped hands, bumped hips and fist bumped again. Alec laughed as the other boy turned to the Skylars. "Secret handshake." He winked at Alec. "Hi. I'm Justin. I work here with Alec."

"Nice to meet you, Justin," said Dr. Skylar. "These are my kids, Luke and Ezzy."

"Uh, hi," stuttered Ezzy, blushing.

"Hey," said Luke, before turning to Ezzy and raising his eyebrows teasingly.

Ezzy punched him in the arm. She'd never been very good around boys, and Luke knew it. All she needed was for him to make her feel even more awkward.

"I'll be helping Alec give you a tour today."

"That's my cue," said Otter. "Thanks, Justin." He turned to Alec. "I'm gonna leave you with Justin to show our friends here the fish farm. Okay?"

Alec nodded while Justin smiled encouragingly.

"Right this way," said Justin, leading the group to the door.

Ezzy followed self-consciously behind the others, trying to act casual and cool, while bracing for the heat. They went down the stairs and crossed the parking lot to one of the long white buildings. Ezzy noticed her father wiping sweat from his forehead. Luke's face began to turn red. At least she wasn't the only one bothered by the South Florida steam bath. Justin didn't seem to even notice it as he strode in front of the group.

At the building's entrance, Justin opened the door and led them inside. He stepped on a wet mat and encouraged them to do the same. "To decontaminate your shoes."

Inside it was cool and the light was dim. Alec ran ahead to a large above-ground round tank. "These are Almaco Jacks," he announced. "They're really curious. Look."

Ezzy stepped up to the tank. A group of gray fish, each about a foot long with a black stripe running along their head, swam toward her. Like kids trying to be first in the lunch line, each fish seemed to be pushing its way to the front of the pack. When a fish stopped by the side of the tank, Ezzy could swear it was looking straight up at her.

"These are the breeding stock," said Alec. "When they spawn, we collect it and then put the eggs in a hatching tank."

Ezzy peered at Alec. His demeanor and speech were different than before. As soon as he began talking about the fish, the boy spoke with confidence and looked directly at the group.

"That's right, dude," said Justin. "We collect males and females from the wild. And then we create just the right conditions for them to spawn. The eggs hatch into larvae or babies and we grow them in another area."

Ezzy stared admiringly at Justin. When he looked her way, she turned swiftly to peer at the fish and promptly lost her balance, bumping into the tank. Ezzy felt her face flush as she peered purposefully into the tank, trying to act as if nothing had happened. The water now swirled with fish. They swam swiftly around in circles, periodically stopping at the edge of the tank to peer up. It reminded her of race cars coming in for a pit stop.

"What do they eat?" asked Luke.

Justin turned to Alec. "Want to show them?"

Alec nodded and went to a bench nearby on which sat several large containers. He carefully opened one, took out a scoop, and filled it with pellets from inside the container. Alec then carefully carried the scoop to the pool and tossed in the pellets. "Fish chow."

The water erupted as the fish rushed to the surface to gobble up the pellets. Ezzy immediately thought—like piranhas. She stepped back a bit and kept her hands firmly at her sides.

"You mean like dog chow?" asked Dr. Skylar.

"Yes," said Justin. "We make it here. One of the big issues in fish farming is the feed. If you capture fish to feed the fish, it kinda defeats the purpose. We're working on creating better fish food that uses just a little fish oil along with a plant protein."

Alec nodded again.

"We can't take you into the area where the larvae are raised," said Justin. "The fish are very sensitive at that stage. But we can go to the grow out ponds and greenhouse."

"Greenhouse?" Luke asked.

"You'll see," responded Justin as he led them past

several more above-ground tanks and a crisscrossing network of pipes. He pointed to a row of green pumps and large white cylinders standing vertically against a wall. "Those are part of the recirculating and filtration system. We have a totally closed system here. We don't release anything into the Bay."

"Uh... what about waste from the fish tanks?" asked Ezzy. "What do you do with it?" She was sure Justin couldn't have anything to do with wastewater getting into the groundwater, but still she wanted to ask. After all, she'd told the Smiths she'd stay on the lookout for anything suspicious. Ezzy tried to act casual as if the question had just popped into her mind.

"Yeah," said Luke. "What do you do with all the fish poop?"

Justin laughed. "We use it to grow vegetables."

Eeuw, thought Ezzy.

"What kind of vegetables?" asked Luke.

"Sea vegetables," said Alec.

"Sea vegetables?"

"Come on," said Alec running toward a door at the far end of the building.

The group followed. After crossing a short grass-lined alleyway, they entered another long white rect-angular building.

Justin pointed to more round above-ground tanks. "These are the grow out tanks. Once the fish get big enough, we sell them to local restaurants and a nearby seafood market. We're trying to prevent overfishing of wild fish."

"Awesome," said Luke.

Justin then walked over to a series of pipes that converged into a chute-like spillway going from the tank area into an attached greenhouse. "The wastewater from the tanks goes into the greenhouse. C'mon." He led them through a glass door directly into the adjacent greenhouse.

Ezzy was so busy watching Justin's corkscrew curls bounce as he walked, she ran into Luke when they stopped just inside the greenhouse. "Sorry."

Luke smirked at her and again raised his eyebrows teasingly.

Ezzy again punched him in the arm.

"Hey."

"Well, whatever you're doing," said Dr. Skylar. "It's definitely working."

Ezzy had to agree. The inside of the greenhouse resembled a well-organized jungle. A lush tangle of green plants rose from rows of white flume-like tanks running the length of the greenhouse. Ezzy looked closer but didn't recognize any of the plants.

"What are they?" Luke asked.

"Like Alec said, dude, they're sea vegetables," answered Justin.

"Huh?" said Luke. "I've never heard of sea vegetables."

Alec walked over to one of the long shallow tanks. "It's saltwater."

Justin joined him and plucked a wrinkled deep-green frond from a circular hole in a covering over the water in the tank. "That's right. This one's kale. It's a special type that can grow in saltwater. Over in the next tank is purslane."

"Purslane?" said Ezzy. "What's that?"

"It's a relative of spinach, but more crunchy," Justin answered.

Nearby, on a small table, was a bowl filled with a leafy green mixture. Justin strode to the table and picked out a handful. "We also have a hybrid lettuce were working on. Here's a mix of some of our greens. Try some." He held out a handful.

Dr. Skylar took a few leaves and popped them into his mouth. "Nice."

Luke tried a piece and smiled. "Kinda salty."

Ezzy smiled shyly and tried to act natural as she took a piece from Justin's hand. She was about to pop it into her mouth, then hesitated. She turned to look back toward the fish tanks where the growing water was coming from. "Uh, you're growing it in fish poop, right?"

"Hey," Justin said. "Some gardeners use horse manure as fertilizer."

Ezzy turned to her father, squinching up her nose.

Dr. Skylar grinned and neighing like a horse said,

"Theyyyyy do."

Ezzy rolled her eyes. She wanted to taste the greens in front of Justin. But the thought of eating something grown in fish poop made her reconsider it. No, this was brave Ezzy, she once again said to herself. She tentatively put a leafy piece into her mouth and chewed. "Yum?"

"We're also growing a variety of algae and sea-weeds," Justin told her. "Did you know that one of the thickeners in ice cream comes from red algae?"

"Algae in ice cream?" Ezzy said.

"It's in there all right," said Justin. "But you can't taste it or anything."

Alec grabbed Justin's hand and pulled him to a door leading outside. "Let's show them the other fish."

Ezzy looked around for pipes or leaks that could be carrying or releasing wastewater into the ground. So far, nothing suspicious, but she vowed to stay on the lookout, even with Justin involved.

* * *

The Undead

After entering the next building, Alec ran to the first in a series of raised rectangular tanks, each about two feet long and six inches deep. "These are the best."

Ezzy caught up and peered into the tank. Swimming about were a bunch of cute inch-long orange fish with wide white stripes. Their fluttery fins and little bodies made their movements sort of a combo wiggle-swim.

"Clownfish," observed Luke. "Right? Like in *Finding Nemo*."

Alec nodded enthusiastically before moving to another row of tanks. "Yellow tangs."

Ezzy and the others followed. The small fish Alec now pointed to were round and bright lemon-yellow.

He ran to the next set of tanks and waved the others over. "Look at these."

When Ezzy caught up and peered into the tank, her eyes grew wide. She gasped. The fish inside were about three inches long, red and white striped, with frilly spines on their fins and along their backs. "Those are lionfish."

"Yes," Justin said.

Luke frowned. "But they're invasive. Why are you growing them?"

"The other fish we're growing are for the aquarium trade," responded Justin, "so people don't collect them from the reefs. But we're growing lionfish to help control the population. We're trying to teach groupers and sharks to eat them. We keep the bigger fish hungry hoping they'll start to eat the lionfish. And in the lab, the scientists are working on a way to pass on a gene so that the lionfish can't reproduce."

"But why grow them?" asked Luke. "Why don't you just catch them?"

"The scientists need to grow them to do their work," answered Justin. "And we use the small ones they produce with the groupers and sharks."

Something clicked in Ezzy's brain. "Did you say lab? Experimenting with lionfish?"

"Yeah," responded Justin. "It's pretty cool."

Luke turned to Ezzy giving her the I-know-exactly-what-you're-thinking look. "Have any of the lionfish from the lab *escaped?*"

"No," answered Justin.

"Have any been released?" asked Ezzy.

"I don't think so. Why?"

Dr. Skylar gestured toward his kids. "These two had a bad experience with some rather large lionfish during a visit to the Aquarius Sea Station."

"Not just large," groaned Ezzy. "*Giant* creepy lionfish that attacked us." She had already decided the incident had probably set her back at least a year on getting over her wild animal phobia.

"Are you sure they were lionfish?" Justin asked.

Ezzy and Luke explained what happened and that they were confident the fish were indeed lionfish.

"Are you sure none of the experimental lionfish have gotten out?" Dr. Skylar repeated.

"Even if they did. I don't see how they'd get that big."

"Maybe we should have a little chat with the scientists," suggested Dr. Skylar. "You know the old saying. Don't mess with Mother Nature."

"They don't like to be bothered," offered Justin.

"When we explain what happened. I suspect they'll be willing to talk with us."

"Okay," said Justin. "But don't say I didn't warn you."

Justin reluctantly led the group past another row of tanks to a glass double door. He punched in a code on a keypad nearby. Ezzy heard a click as the door opened, and he walked through, leading them up a flight of stairs to another glass doorway. Justin knocked. Inside, a pale stocky man in a white lab coat turned and held up a hand acknowledging their presence. He had black hair flecked with gray and a matching tuft on his chin. Narrowing his eyes, the man stared at Justin and the group, shaking his head. He spoke to a young woman also wearing a white lab coat before walking over. He punched in a keycode and Ezzy heard a click as the door swung open.

"Justin," said the man. "I believe I said *no* unscheduled tours."

Dr. Skylar stepped forward. "Hello, my name is Dr. Ben Skylar, and these are my kids, Ezzy and Luke."

"I'm sure you are very lovely people, but I'm working on something important right now."

Ezzy didn't like the man's high and mighty tone.

"I think what we have to say is, in fact, rather important," said Dr. Skylar.

You go Dad, thought Ezzy.

The scientist glared at Dr. Skylar.

"Some of the fish from your lab may have escaped into the ocean."

"What?" said the scientist. "That's not possible."

"Is there someplace we could speak for a few minutes?"

The scientist hesitated. "I suppose so. There's a

small conference room inside. But I can only spare a few minutes. Follow me and don't touch *anything.*"

He led them around the outskirts of the lab into a room with a modern silver and glass conference table and six matching chairs. Along the way, Ezzy checked out the lab. There were microscopes, dissecting pans, and computers along with a bunch of high-tech equipment she didn't recognize. Shelving on one side of the room held numerous aquariums. The tanks contained an assortment of small colorful fish.

"Have a seat," said the scientist. "My name is Dr. Mudbourne."

"Mudbourne?" blurted out Luke.

"Yes, *Dr.* Mudbourne," grunted the man. "Now what's this all about?"

Dr. Skylar proceeded to explain about the giant lionfish at the Aquarius Sea Station.

"So?" said Dr. Mudbourne. "There are a lot of lionfish out there."

"They don't usually get that big," said Luke.

"Or attack people," added Ezzy.

"What are you implying?"

"We're not implying anything," Dr. Skylar replied. "We'd just like to ask you a few questions."

"Like what?"

"Like what are you doing to the lionfish?" Luke said. "And did any escape?"

Ezzy remembered again how after their mother died, Luke was shy for a long time. He hardly ever spoke in public. She kinda wished a little bit of that Luke was left. Now he had a habit of blurting out whatever he was thinking.

"First of all, young man," said Dr. Mudbourne. "We have not released any of our lionfish into the ocean or onto the reef. And secondly, we are not creating giant lionfish. We're simply modifying them to pass on a gene so that their eggs are not viable. Eventually, then, the fish out there will become sterile."

Justin raised his hand as if they were in a classroom. "You know, some of the small lionfish we use to train the sharks and groupers are kinda aggressive."

Alec raised his hand. "They eat a lot."

The scientist glared at Justin and Alec. "Lionfish are known to be slightly aggressive and so what if they eat a lot."

"Could an increased growth rate and amped-up aggression be a side effect of what you're doing?" asked Dr. Skylar.

"I suppose that's possible," responded Dr. Mudbourne. "But as I said before, we've never released any and as far as I know, none have escaped." He turned again to Justin and Alec. "Right boys?"

Alec nodded, but Justin hesitated. "Uh... well... we haven't released any *live* lionfish."

"What's that supposed to mean?" the scientist asked.

Justin hesitated. "Well... you know how we're trying to train the groupers and sharks to eat lionfish. And they need to be alive."

"Yes."

"And sometimes the lionfish die, either in the tanks or the ones you give us to dispose of from the lab."

"Yes."

Justin looked briefly at Alec who stared pointedly at the floor. "We... I mean I... didn't think it would matter. We've been sort of giving them a burial at sea."

Luke looked confused. "What does that mean?"

"We... uh... dump the dead lionfish in the canal by the dock. But they're dead."

"You what?" asked the scientist, his face turning scarlet.

"We felt bad for them and figured they were dead, so it didn't matter," said Justin. "But there was this one time that... well, six fish kinda disappeared right after we dumped them. We thought something probably ate them. But maybe..."

"Maybe what?" asked Dr. Skylar.

"Maybe they weren't as dead as we thought."

"Undead lionfish?" said Luke. "Like zombie lionfish?"

Ezzy rolled her eyes at her brother. "You've been watching way too many mummy and zombie movies. Maybe they just looked dead but weren't."

Dr. Mudbourne turned to Justin and Alec. If looks could kill, Ezzy thought the man was about to commit murder. He took a breath clearly trying to stem his anger. "We'll discuss this and your jobs later, boys." He looked to Ezzy and Luke. "Okay, where are the lionfish you saw now?"

"They've disappeared," Ezzy answered.

Dr. Mudbourne sighed. "Well, then maybe it's nothing to worry about."

"Unless they come back and attack more people," countered Luke.

"They did put one diver in the hospital," Dr. Skyler told the scientist. "He's going to be okay, but still. Those fish need to be found and caught."

Dr. Mudbourne eyed the group around the table. "There's no real evidence that these fish came from my lab."

"Where else would they come from?" Luke blurted out.

"Yeah," added Ezzy.

"Mutations happen all the time in nature," Dr. Mudbourne offered.

"Come on," said Dr. Skylar. "We both know the most likely explanation is that they are genetically modified lionfish from your lab."

"I suppose it's possible," Dr. Mudbourne said. "What would it take to keep all of you quiet about the possible connection to the lab?"

"What?" Luke responded.

"Fat chance," said Ezzy. "Those things almost killed us."

"Look," said Dr. Skylar. "Let's not panic. I am sure Dr. Mudbourne is not suggesting we ignore the issue." He turned to the man.

"No, of course not. I'm just saying I could use a little time to confirm where the fish came from. I'd hate for people in the community to get the wrong idea about my work here. We're trying to help, not cause problems."

"Well," said Dr. Skylar. "Maybe if you could help figure out how to deal with the situation, it would negate any hard feelings in the community if the large lionfish *did* come from your lab."

"*Giant*, Dad," said Ezzy. "*Giant*, creepy, mean lionfish."

A new look came across the scientist's face, as if he'd just realized something. "Hmmm. Maybe we can cut a deal?"

Ezzy didn't like the sound of that.

"What sort of deal?" asked Dr. Skylar.

"I know how we can find and capture the lionfish. And if we capture them, I can not only see if they came from here, I could also study them to learn more about why they're so big."

"Where else would a mutant giant aggressive lionfish come from?" stated Luke.

"Yeah," added Ezzy again.

The scientist glared at them. "I'm just saying, I have unique knowledge and experience that could be vital to capturing the fish. More than anyone else."

Dr. Skylar paused before answering. "What do you want from us in this so-called deal?"

"To let me capture the fish and confirm that they are or are not from my lab. And not tell anyone about the possible connection to the lab until it has been confirmed one way or the other."

"Whaaat?" said Ezzy.

Luke shook his head.

"Look, I am the only one who can quickly find these fish," announced Dr. Mudbourne.

"What exactly are you suggesting?" asked Dr. Skylar.

Dr. Mudbourne gave them a brief overview of his plan.

"Can you give us more specifics? I mean, even if the lionfish are territorial and tend to stay in one general area, how exactly are you going to find them?"

"For now, just know that with all my years of research, I know more about these fish than anyone. I am the world's expert. I have a way to do it."

Oh brother, Ezzy thought. Does this guy have a big head or what?

After a few more questions, Dr. Skylar reluctantly agreed to wait to tell anyone else about the possible connection to the lab. He then called the sea station base to let Otter know they were going out on a short cruise with the fish farm staff. Since Alec often went out with them, Otter simply thanked him for the heads-up and said he'd see them later.

*   *   *

Love Potion #9

E zzy peered over the side of the boat as it cruised north past the multi-million-dollar homes and red mangroves lining the shore of Florida Bay. In the shallow water below were beds of wide-bladed seagrass and round black sponge resembling rubber tires. Her father had reluctantly agreed to go along and not say anything as long as there was no risk to the kids. Ezzy was excited yet nervous. She didn't like Dr. Mudbourne but was glad to go along and be part of the team trying to find the monster lionfish—given the assurance she wouldn't have to get in the water.

Sitting beside Luke and her father on a bench seat, Ezzy watched as Dr. Mudbourne's divers prepared their gear. She turned toward the boat's unusual stern where a seawater-filled tank had been built into the deck.

To be heard over the boat's inboard engine, Dr. Skylar had to shout. "Dr. Mudbourne, I still think we should have told Otter and asked for their help."

"I've got all the help we need," the man replied. He had exchanged his white lab coat for a gaudy Hawaiian button-down shirt, khaki shorts, and a floppy hat. Ezzy figured it was his tourist imposter get-up.

Sitting beside the Skylars were Alec and Justin.

"At the least, we should have left the kids back at the lab," noted Dr. Skylar.

"They'll be fine," replied Dr. Mudbourne. "Alec and Justin regularly go out on the boat. It's no big deal. Right guys?"

Justin gave Alec's hand a squeeze. "Yeah, we do go out. But never to hunt down big lionfish."

"I keep telling you. Make that *creepy, mean, giant* lionfish," said Ezzy.

"Can you tell us more about your plan?" asked Dr. Skylar. "Like how exactly you're going to attract or find the lionfish."

"I'll explain once we get on site."

Ezzy had been wondering the same thing. The only additional information they'd gotten was from the captain who had given them an extremely brief safety talk when they boarded, explaining where the lifejackets were if they needed to abandon ship. Ezzy hoped that wasn't in her near future. Then again, given her and Luke's history, she figured it was a definite possibility.

The captain stood at the helm. He was a petite but hardened man with stiff graying hair and intense dark brown eyes. He maneuvered the boat into a canal that cut through the limestone underlying Key Largo and connected Florida Bay to the Atlantic Ocean.

"Hey, check that out," said Luke, pointing to a fan-like shape in the canal wall.

"Coral," said Alec, looking up.

"That's right," added Justin. "The Florida Keys are made up of the remains of a coral reef that grew when sea level was higher about 125,000 years ago. You can see the old coral skeletons in the limestone walls of the canal and in some of the buildings built from a local quarry."

"Wow," said Luke.

Ezzy shrugged. She was more interested in how the heck they were going to find and capture the scary lionfish. She watched the divers checking several spearguns and the specialized underwater dart guns Dr. Mudbourne had told them about as part of his plan. She turned to Justin. He didn't look as confident as earlier.

Going with the outflowing tide, the boat cruised quickly through the canal and into the open ocean. Soon the wind picked up and waves rocked the boat. Atop the tank in the deck, small waves sloshed back and forth. Ezzy thought it was like a miniature storm in the water-filled compartment.

"Might be a little bouncy," noted the captain.

Luke smiled and raised his arms as if on a roller-coaster. "Whoohoo! No hands."

Ezzy shook her head. Go figure. Luke got motion sick on almost any vehicle except a boat. She turned from her brother to watch the water rush by. A cool breeze from the boat's motion lessened the day's heat and humidity. A few deep-sea fishing and dive boats passed, some heading back to land, others offshore. The ocean had gone from a murky green to deep blue. Ezzy looked skyward. A few gray clouds drifted by. They reminded her of the impending storm. She wondered how far away it was. She turned to the south. The ocean stretched clear to the horizon. There, the cloud cover grew more solid, darker and ominous. Ezzy tried not to think about the storm; they had enough to worry about already. Namely six giant mutant lionfish.

Some twenty minutes later, the captain slowed the boat and turned into the waves. Ezzy watched as one of the divers made his way to the bow. He grabbed a boat hook and stood at the rail, balancing as the deck heaved up and down. As the boat glided to a halt, the diver reached down toward a mooring buoy. Seconds later, he stood up with a looped line around the boat hook. "Got it," he yelled, securing the line around a cleat.

The captain shut off the engine and turned to Dr. Mudbourne. "We're onsite as requested. Have a couple of hours before the seas begin to pick up."

The scientist nodded and turned to the divers. "Now remember, we want to capture the lionfish and put them in the well in the deck. It should be big enough to transport them to the lab. And..."

"In there?" Luke interrupted pointing to the tank. "They're really big. No way they'll fit in there."

"Not a chance," added Ezzy.

The scientist stared at the two as if his one wish in the world was to hold a sword to their backs and make them walk the plank. "As I was about to say before being rudely interrupted. I brought a concentrated form of Rotenone in the darts to anesthetize the fish." He turned directly to Luke. "And yes, even very big fish. Then we can put them in the well until we reach the lab."

"All of them?" asked Dr. Skylar.

"Yes."

"Nope," said Luke.

"Double nope," added Ezzy.

Ezzy noticed Justin stifle a laugh and beamed.

"We'll see," said Dr. Mudbourne, nodding to the divers who were pulling on their full-length black wetsuits.

"Besides," said Ezzy. "How are you going to get them? No one knows where they are."

The scientist turned to Dr. Skylar. "Do your children always interrupt and ask so many questions?"

"You have no idea," he replied. "But thankfully, yes."

The scientist tapped his head as if it held all the answers. "As I have already told you, I know a lot more about these fish than you or anyone, and I have something that should do the trick."

"What?" asked Luke.

The scientist rolled his eyes and shook his head. "Fish release pheromones or chemicals when they are threatened, injured or if they want to attract mates. This has been part of my research for years." The man reached into a small cooler at his feet and took out a plastic container about the size of a water flask along with a syringe. "We'll release a few ounces of this lion-fish love potion into the water, and they should quickly show up. Chemicals spread rapidly in the sea and fish can sense them from very far away."

"Kinda like sharks and blood?" asked Luke.

"You had to bring up sharks," Ezzy said.

"One of the divers will go down and release the pheromones at depth," said Dr. Mudbourne. "Then we'll give it some time to work before the full team goes down to anesthetize and capture the fish."

"What if the darts don't work?" asked Ezzy. "I mean they're big and mean."

"If we can't capture them, then I'll leave their fate to the divers. I just need at least one, preferably alive and unharmed."

Ezzy looked to the divers, where the leader hoisted a speargun and said, "No worries there."

"What would you like us to do?" asked Dr. Skylar.

"Stay out of the way," the scientist responded. "Then again, can you snorkel? We could use some spotters in the water at the surface. I have a hydrophone to alert the divers if the fish are seen from above."

Ezzy vigorously shook her head. "Nope. Nope. Not going in there with those mutant lionfish. Not going to happen."

"Me either," added Luke.

"Or me," said Dr. Skylar.

"I thought you wanted to get rid of these fish?" grunted Dr. Mudbourne. "Besides, you'll be safe on the surface."

"Famous last words," noted Ezzy. "Nope, not going to happen."

"No risk to the kids," said Dr. Skylar. "That was the deal. We should have brought more divers from the Aquarius staff."

Dr. Mudbourne turned to Justin and Alec. "You two work for me and if they are from the lab, it's kind of your fault this all happened. You can be the spotters in the water."

"Don't do it," urged Ezzy.

Justin nodded. "Dude, I'll do it, but I think Alec should stay up here."

"I thought he was good in the water," said the scientist. "At least that's what you've been assuring me."

"He is, but this could be dangerous."

"No," said Alec. "I'll do it."

Dr. Skylar turned to the boy. "This is not your fault, and you don't have to do it, Alec. You can stay up here with us."

The boy shook his head. "I want to help. I'll go in."

*   *   *

The Chase Is On

E zzy tried again to convince Alec not to go in the water. But after a diver returned from dispersing the lionfish-attracting chemicals below, he readied his fins, mask, and snorkel.

"Dad," said Ezzy. "Say something so he doesn't go in."

Dr. Mudbourne stepped forward. "He'll be fine on the surface. Stop interfering. We had a deal."

"We'll watch closely from up here," Dr. Skylar assured Ezzy. "If it looks like it's getting dangerous, we'll get both of them out of the water."

Ezzy grimaced. She had a bad feeling about this whole operation. She wondered if there was something

Dr. Mudbourne wasn't telling them.

"We are about due south of the Aquarius Sea Station, and the current is flowing north today," explained Dr. Mudbourne. "So, if those fish are still in the vicinity of the undersea lab, they should quickly sense the attracting agent and swim toward the place where it originated. Which would be here, below the boat."

Putting a long rod-like instrument over the side and lashing it to a cleat near the stern, the captain addressed the team. "The hydrophone's in. We'll test it when you're down. If the spotters overhead see the lionfish, we'll send out a ping and give you a heading."

"Roger that," said the lead diver, handing gloves to the other divers. "They're Kevlar. Should protect us from the spines and toxin. But be careful, these fish are not oversized damselfish, they could do some damage."

"Okay," announced Dr. Mudbourne. "I think you'd better get in."

Fully suited up, one by one the divers made their way to the stern platform and did a giant stride into the water. The captain handed each a dart and speargun. The team then descended and were soon out of sight. Outfitted for snorkeling, Justin and Alec made their way to the stern.

"Good to go, dude?" Justin asked Alec.

He nodded.

"Let's stay together and near the boat. If you see anything let me know right away."

"Be careful," Dr. Skylar told them. "Get back in the boat if you don't feel safe."

"They'll be fine," assured Dr. Mudbourne.

Ezzy watched closely as Justin and Alec jumped in and floated at the surface behind the boat. She wished she could have convinced them not to go in.

The captain tied a long line to a cleat at the stern and threw an attached buoy overboard. It streamed out behind the boat, near the two boys snorkeling. He then moved to a small yellow waterproof box connected to the hydrophone he'd deployed earlier and put on a headset. Grinning, he connected his phone to the control box and turned to the others. "This will be a good test." After a few taps here and there, the captain watched the snorkelers with anticipation.

Almost immediately, Justin looked up at the group aboard the boat and spit out his snorkel. "That's not funny. We're already talking mutant mean fish."

Alec raised an arm and gave a thumbs up.

"What's he talking about?" asked Luke.

The captain replied with a devilish smirk, "Just testing the hydrophone. Piped down the music from the movie *Jaws* to see if they could hear it. You know, the dunt... dunt... part. Looks like it's working good."

"Awesome," said Luke chuckling.

"Not awesome," countered Ezzy. "That's just mean. Bad enough they're waiting for killer lionfish to show up and you do that."

"Lighten up, sweetie," said the captain. "They'll be fine. Those divers down there live, eat, and breathe this stuff."

"How's the visibility?" shouted Dr. Mudbourne to Justin and Alec.

"Clear to the bottom, about thirty feet I think," responded Justin. "We can see the divers and patch reefs. Nothing yet."

Alec and Justin kicked slowly, circling behind the boat and scanning the area below. Standing beside their father at the stern, Ezzy and Luke watched their every move. The captain sat on a bench with his feet up, headset on, and eyes closed.

Ezzy fidgeted as the minutes ticked by. The silence on the boat was jarring. Picturing the giant lionfish in her mind, she wanted to scream for Alec and Justin to get out.

Moments later, Alec grunted through his snorkel. Justin grabbed the boy's arm, pushed him toward the stern of the boat, and spit out his snorkel. "Giant lionfish coming in from the north."

The captain sat up, tapped on the hydrophone controls before speaking into the headset microphone. "Lionfish coming in from the north."

"Do the divers see them?" Ezzy asked Alec who was now hanging onto the dive platform.

He didn't answer.

"Two more coming from the west," shouted Justin.

Alec jumped up and swung around to sit on the platform, while Justin stayed floating behind the boat. Dr. Skylar took the boy's fins and helped him into the boat. "Good choice, Alec."

"What's happening?" shouted Dr. Mudbourne.

Justin kicked to the left, made a sharp turn, and swam back.

"Are the divers okay?" yelled Dr. Skylar.

Justin looked up. "I'm not sure who's chasing who down there. I think they're having trouble with the darts." He put his snorkel back in his mouth, peered down and kicked, moving quickly about twenty-five yards to the north.

"Stay closer," shouted Ezzy, wringing her hands.

Luke smirked at Ezzy. "You like him."

"Shut up."

Justin then raced back to the stern. He leapt up to a seated position on the dive platform before climbing into the boat. "They're coming up. Not sure if they darted any of the fish."

Dr. Skylar waved to Ezzy, Luke, and Alec. "Move back."

One of the divers popped up right behind the dive platform and spit out his regulator. He took off his fins and began climbing up the ladder to the side of the platform. "Not sure about these darts or if we got any of them. Tough suckers. Once we started shooting them, they veered away fast or came at us. Had to fend them off with the spears. Tried hitting a couple, but they were too quick."

The other two divers surfaced at the base of the ladder. One climbed up as the other handed his tank up to the first diver and heaved himself up onto platform.

"Man, those things are fast *and mean*," said the last diver. "Never seen anything like it. I got a couple darts off, but don't know if I hit any."

"What?" said Dr. Mudbourne. "They all got away?"

"Sorry Doc.," said the lead diver. "I think we need to rethink our strategy." He looked at the well in the boat. "Besides if we do catch even one, I agree with the kids here. It's not gonna fit in there."

"Whoa!" shouted Luke, pointing behind the boat.

"What?" said the group in unison, turning to see what he was pointing to.

"Holy giant lionfish!" said Dr. Skylar.

"I think you got one," said Ezzy, staring wide-eyed at the enormous lionfish that had floated to the surface and lay still, belly-up.

"Is it dead?" Luke asked.

"Or undead?" said Ezzy.

"Must have hit one with a dart after all," said Dr. Mudbourne. "Should be out for a while. Let's get it into the boat."

Ezzy shook her head. "How about... just leaving it there?"

Dr. Mudbourne nearly shoved her out of the way as he strode to the stern. "Come on, let's get it in."

The captain brought forward a large hook on a stick.

Dr. Mudbourne stood to the side. "Don't injure it."

"Injure it?" said the captain. "I'm hoping it's already dead."

"Or undead," added Luke.

"Hang on," said the captain as he put the hooked gaff down and pulled in the line floating behind the stern. "We might be able to snag it with the buoy and pull it closer." He coiled the line and threw the buoy out over the floating lionfish. He then slowly pulled the line and buoy toward the boat. "Here little fishy," he said chuckling.

Soon the lionfish lay next to the dive platform, floating motionless. Ezzy leaned closer to see it better. The captain grabbed the gaff. "I'll hook it and drag it onto the dive platform. Let's be sure it's either fully knocked out or dead."

Seeing the size of the fish and its poison-filled spines, Ezzy decided capturing even one and having it alive on the boat seemed like a really bad idea. "I vote for dead. Really dead."

To her surprise, Luke nodded. Even her animal-lover brother realized these fish needed to be permanently done away with.

Dr. Mudbourne scowled at them.

The captain climbed onto the dive platform and poked the enormous lionfish with the gaff. It bobbed up and down and rolled over a bit but remained still, floating at the surface. "It's either asleep or dead all right." He hooked the fish and began to drag it up onto the platform.

Two divers wearing Kevlar gloves climbed onto the dive platform to help the captain. The others stood at the stern, leaning over to watch.

"Careful," ordered Dr. Mudbourne. "Try not to damage it."

The fish was at least five feet in length. Its wide frilly dorsal and pectoral fins made it look even larger. The divers and captain were able to get about half the fish up onto the platform. The rest hung down in the water. As they began to pull it further up, Ezzy noticed motion in the water behind the fish. She again leaned closer to see better. Suddenly, the ocean exploded upward, and a loud chomp resounded. The divers let go of the fish and leapt into the boat. Ezzy reeled backward, pulling Luke with her.

"Shark!" shouted one of the divers.

Still shaken, but driven by curiosity, Ezzy crept cautiously back to the stern. Hanging off the dive platform with half the lionfish in its mouth was a huge gray shark. The captain stood frozen nearby still holding the gaff in the lionfish's mouth. Ezzy watched as the shark bit through the lionfish and sank out of sight, taking half the lionfish with it.

"Whoa!" said Luke, now standing beside Ezzy.

"Crud," shouted Dr. Mudbourne. "Save the rest of the fish!"

The captain shrugged, looking at what was left of the lionfish. "Uh, sorry Doc. But I think it got a little damaged." He chuckled then shook his head. "Happens a lot out here. Catch a fish and then a shark or barracuda gets most of it."

Ezzy grimaced and shook her head. "That was horrible."

Dr. Skylar put his arm around her. "It's okay honey. No one was hurt and the shark is gone."

"Yeah, but I will never unsee that. I think it's seared into my brain forever."

Luke nodded, but not with a look of horror. "It was awesome."

Ezzy lightly punched him in the arm. "You are truly sick."

"Come on, boys," ordered the captain. "Let's get the rest of this thing in before someone else comes up for a bite."

While the Skylars, Alec, and Justin moved away from the stern, the dive team and captain hauled what was left of the lionfish into the boat.

"No point in putting it in the live well," said the lead diver. "Let's just strap it down in the stern for the ride in."

"What about the other lionfish?" asked Dr. Skylar.

"They're dangerous. We can't just leave them."

Both Ezzy and Luke nodded.

The captain turned to the south, staring at the horizon. "With all the action, you may not have noticed those dark clouds or the wind picking up. Storm's a comin' and seas are going to get rough. We need to head in."

"What about the lionfish?" Luke repeated.

"After the storm," said the lead diver. "We can try again. And this will give us time to think up a new strategy." He threw one of the dart guns into a bucket. "These things aren't going to cut it."

Dr. Skylar pointed to the lionfish head at the stern. "Dr. Mudbourne, is that enough to determine if it came from your lab?"

He shrugged. "Won't know until I do a genetic analysis. So please don't say anything to anyone. And since no one will be out diving during the storm, there shouldn't be any problems for a day or so at least. I'll know by then for sure and if needed, I can come up with a new plan to get the rest."

"To kill them?" Ezzy asked.

The scientist nodded noncommittally.

The captain started the engine. One of the divers went to the bow.

"Okay, release it," shouted the captain. The diver released the mooring line. As soon as the boat was free, it drifted back. The captain put the vessel in gear and turned toward shore. Ezzy and the others sat down on the benches along the rail and held on. The deck rolled and rocked. Dr. Mudbourne stared at the fish head. Ezzy wondered what he was thinking. She turned to her father. "What now?"

"We head back and hunker down for the storm," he answered, and then lowering his voice added, "and I think it's time to tell the Aquarius team what's going on."

*   *   *

Hurricane Jose

Otter arrived at the fish farm to drive the group back to sea station headquarters. As soon as they got into the SUV, he turned to his son. "How'd it go?"

Alec stared pointedly at his feet. "Okay."

Otter's brow furrowed. "How was the boat ride?"

"Okay."

"Did something happen?" Otter turned to Dr. Skylar in the passenger seat. "Did everything go all right?"

"That depends on your definition of all right, I think," he replied. "We've got some things to tell you regarding the fish farm and those big lionfish. But let's wait until we get back."

Otter cocked his head curiously. "Sure. We can do that."

No one spoke for the rest of the ride. After parking the car, Otter led the way into the briefing room. "Take a seat and tell me what happened."

The Skylars sat on one couch and Alec sat on a chair near his father.

There was an awkward silence until Luke blurted out. "The lionfish came from the lab at the fish farm."

"Whaat?" responded Otter.

"Did you know they've been genetically modifying lionfish there?" asked Dr. Skylar.

"Not really," Otter replied. "Alec told me they were teaching grouper and sharks to eat them, but not much else."

Alec looked at his father and nodded.

"They're also trying to make them sterile," said Dr. Skylar. "The plan was to then release them so they could pass on the gene and prevent the invasive ones from reproducing."

"That sounds like a pretty good idea," Otter said.

"Yeah, except they get big and mean too," said Ezzy.

"That's not good," Otter noted. "But my understanding is they haven't released any fish into the ocean. Right Alec?"

Alec stared at his feet and whispered, "Not on purpose."

"What does that mean?"

"None have been released officially," said Dr. Sky-lar. "But looks like Alec and Justin dumped some fish they thought were dead into a canal."

"But they were undead," added Luke.

"They weren't really dead," explained Ezzy. Notic-ing that Alec looked about to cry, she added, "It was an accident."

Otter squatted next to Alec and took his face in his hands. "Alec, it's okay. It was an accident. You didn't know they weren't dead."

"Yeah," said Ezzy. "If it's anyone's fault, it's that Dr. Mudbourne guy."

"I am not sure it's anyone's fault," said her father. "Sometimes things really are just accidents. Dr. Mud-bourne's work has been for a good purpose. They're trying to help solve the problem of the invasive lion-fish. He didn't order the fish released or anything."

"But then how come he didn't seem like he wanted to kill the ones that attacked us and are still out there?" asked Ezzy.

"I'm not sure that's true," her father replied. "He just wanted to catch the fish so that he could study them and confirm they came from his lab."

"Catch them?" said Otter. "I think you better tell me exactly what happened over there today."

The Skylars recounted their day at the fish farm and how it led to a trip out to the reef. Otter sat listening quietly. When they'd finished, he shook his head and turned to Alec. "If I had known what Dr.

Mudbourne was up to, no way you would have been out there. You should have called me."

Alec nodded. "I know, Dad. Sorry."

"And you, Dr. Skylar," said Otter. "How could you let the kids go out with them?"

"I'm sorry, Otter," he replied. "You're right. I'm not making excuses, but Dr. Mudbourne was very convincing that he had special knowledge and a plan that if we didn't tell anyone about the possible connection to his lab and went with him, would be our best chance of catching those fish. And even now, he hasn't actually confirmed genetically that the lionfish came from his lab."

"Duh," said Ezzy. "Where else would they come from."

"But that's why we're telling you now," continued Dr. Skylar. "He got one of the fish, but there are still five out there. He and his divers are going to come up with a new plan. But I think they could use your help."

"Five? Are you sure that's all?" Otter asked.

"According to the boys," Dr. Skylar answered. "There were six lionfish that they dumped that might not have been dead. And one has been caught."

"Do we know if they can reproduce?" Otter asked. "Could there be baby monster mutant lionfish out there too?"

Ezzy cringed. She hadn't thought about that.

"That's a good, but worrying question," said Dr. Skylar. "We'd better ask Dr. Mudbourne about it. I'll try to give him a call. Do you have the number for the fish farm?"

"Sure," said Otter. "But like everyone else, the folks there may be busy preparing for the storm. It's come off Cuba, entered the warm waters of the Gulf Stream and looks like it's going to strengthen. The forecast has it headed north skirting the coast as a Cat one hurricane. Hurricane Jose."

"Did someone say hurricane?" asked Phil Smith as he and his wife strode into the room. They still wore their old-age outfits but had dumped their canes and elderly demeanor.

"Yes," said Otter. "Looks like the storm is heading this way and will be a Cat one when it passes by just offshore very early tomorrow morning."

"Could it wobble?" asked Luke.

"Wobble?" asked Otter. "We worry about that, but how'd you know about it?"

"He reads and remembers everything," noted Ezzy.

Luke grinned. "Yeah, and I remember a storm, I think it was named Charlie, it wobbled and hit the other side of Florida unexpectedly."

Otter nodded. "Not really unexpectedly. The problem is that people were paying too much attention to the middle line in the forecast cone. The entire area was under a warning. But to answer your question.

Yes, if the storm *wobbles*, it could hit us directly. That's why we're battening down the hatches."

"What if it rapidly intensifies?" asked Luke.

"Young Luke here seems to have the makings of a meteorologist," said Phil. "Is that what you want to be when you grow up?"

"Maybe," said Luke. "Or a veterinarian or marine biologist. But you know, weather effects animals too."

"Even if the storm intensifies, it still doesn't look like it will be a major hurricane," said Otter. "Our buildings are safe and built to withstand hurricane-strength winds and flooding, which could happen if we get storm surge. We have a generator for mission control and plenty of water and food if the power goes out. So, best to hunker down tonight and stay inside."

Ezzy turned to Phil and Gracie, remembering their mission at the resort. "Hey, what'd you find out? Are they dumping their wastewater?"

Phil turned to Gracie. "My dear. The floor is yours."

Gracie planted a kiss on her husband's cheek. "Thank you, kind sir." She turned to the group. "I am pleased and not so pleased to tell you we found no evidence that they are releasing their wastes illegally or dumping anything."

Ezzy was disappointed. She'd hoped they would discover some evil plot or carelessness that could explain the cause of the algae bloom. "Are you sure? It's not like they're going to advertise it or anything."

Phil smiled at her. "Right you are, young Ezzy. That's just what we were thinking. We have an idea about how we might make sure their wastewater is not contaminating the groundwater and leaking out on the reefs."

"You do?" said Ezzy.

"Yes," answered Gracie. "We've already consulted with Professor Miller. After the storm, we're going to release some dye into the resort's wastewater stream, and she is going to put a sensor down that can detect even very small amounts of dye if it comes out at the deep reef."

Dr. Skylar raised his hand. "Uh, how are you going to get the dye into their waste stream?"

"That's where you two come in," Gracie said to Ezzy and Luke.

"Us?" said Luke.

"If it's okay with your dad, of course," said Phil.

"Can we, Dad?" asked Ezzy.

"Let me get the details and then we can decide."

"Cool," said Ezzy.

"What about the lionfish?" asked Luke.

"What about them?" said Gracie. "Did we miss something?"

The group filled the Smiths in on their adventure at the fish farm and aboard the boat earlier. Soon after, Otter waved his hand to get everyone's attention. "For now, let's focus on getting through the storm. I'll give my pals at Fish and Wildlife a heads up about the possible connection to the lab. I already called them to report the big lionfish incident."

Ezzy shook her head. "Dr. Mudbourne's not gonna like that."

*   *   *

After dinner, the Skylars spent the night in their suite watching coverage of the approaching storm on The Weather Channel. The staff had gone home to ride it out with their families. By 9PM the storm had become Hurricane Jose with sustained winds of 90 miles per hour.

Ezzy scooted closer to her dad and brother on the couch. "It still sounds pretty calm outside."

"If the hurricane stays small and passes offshore," said her father. "Might not be much worse than this."

"Unless it wobbles," offered Luke.

"Unless it wobbles," repeated his father. "But remember what Otter said. These buildings are safe, and they have a generator next door if the power goes out."

Just then, something crashed onto the porch, drawing everyone's attention to the sliding doors. A big palm frond now sat plastered up against the glass.

"I think the wind is picking up," said Ezzy.

Rain began to hammer the roof and slider door.

Dr. Skylar pointed to the radar image on the television. Looks like we're in one of the outer bands of the storm."

"You know," said Luke. "The safest place to be in a hurricane is an interior room like the bathroom."

"That's right," responded his father.

"We should put some water and snacks in the bathroom just in case the storm wobbles and gets stronger."

"Good idea, son. Best to be prepared just in case. You two get some pillows and blankets to put in there and I'll make some snacks. How about the old standard... PB and Js?"

"Sounds good, Dad," said Ezzy, following her brother into their bedroom.

"I'll look for a flashlight too," added Luke. "In case the power goes out."

If she had to be in a hurricane, Ezzy was glad she was with her good-to-be-prepared father and brother.

After they'd put supplies in the bathroom, they regrouped on the couch. On the television a storm specialist was giving an update. "Hurricane Jose remains a Cat one with 95 mile-per-hour sustained winds, moving north northeast at a good clip, 17 miles per hour. The models have it turning more easterly and missing the coast, but it's unclear when the turn will occur."

"Is it going to get stronger?" Luke asked, talking to the television.

"Looks like people in the Florida Keys should expect driving rain, potential moderate flooding from storm surge, and some high winds," said the expert on-air.

Soon the rain and wind outside subsided. Ezzy looked at the radar image on the television. The outer band of the storm had passed.

"How about you two get ready for bed?" Dr. Skylar suggested.

"What about the storm?" Ezzy asked.

"I want to see what it's like when it gets closer," added Luke.

Dr. Skylar paused. "Okay, how about this. You guys put on something comfortable to sleep in. We'll get the pillows and blankets and camp out here and if it starts to get bad, we'll move into the bathroom."

Ezzy and Luke nodded before heading into their room to wash up and change into clothes to sleep in. By the time they returned, their father had piled pillows and blankets on the rug next to the couch and lowered the sound on the television. Luke and Ezzy laid down and watched the progress of the hurricane with their father.

As the outer bands passed and the storm approached, the wind intermittently strengthened, and rain periodically lashed the windows and pelted the roof.

"What about storm surge?" Luke asked sleepily.

"We're on the second floor," his father replied.

"Don't think we need to worry about that."

Ezzy put her head on a pillow. "Wake me up if it wobbles."

"Will do," replied her father.

"I'm gonna stay awake just in case," said Luke with his eyes half closed.

Ezzy snickered quietly, knowing he'd be asleep any minute. Listening to the wind and rain, her eyelids began to droop and soon she dozed off as well.

*   *   *

Keeping It Cool

The next morning, Ezzy woke up atop a bed of blankets on the floor next to her brother. She listened for the wind and rain. But all she heard was the sound of palm fronds rustling in a breeze. She looked out the sliding glass doors. Between puffy white clouds was a patch of blue sky. The storm had passed.

Ezzy thought it seemed a little warm inside. She looked up. The previously rotating ceiling fan sat still. On the nearby couch, her father lay asleep. She nudged Luke who rolled over and muttered, "What?"

"I think the power's out," Ezzy whispered. "Did you get up to see the storm when it was close?"

Luke shook his head. "Dang. Must have slept right through it." He jumped up and went to the sliding glass doors.

"Any damage?" croaked their father, who had opened one eye and lifted his head.

"Only some branches and stuff lying around," answered Luke.

"But I think the power's out," added Ezzy.

Luke tried a light switch. "Yup, power's out."

Dr. Skylar swung his legs around and sat up, rubbing his eyes. "Fell asleep before the storm hit, but I think it turned east sooner than predicted. Probably why it didn't wake us up or hopefully cause much damage."

"Wonder how the Sea Station did underwater?" said Luke.

"Let's have some breakfast and then head over to headquarters to see what's up," said Dr. Skylar. "Lucky we have some Hurricane Jose PB and Js ready to eat."

The Skylars got dressed and had breakfast. A knock on the slider doors drew their attention outside. Phil and Gracie Smith waved through the glass. Dr. Skylar waved back. "Come on in."

Phil slid open the door and Gracie stepped through. "Thought we'd come by to see how you weathered the storm." She looked at Luke and winked. "Weathered... get it?"

Luke chuckled.

"Everything's fine here," said Dr. Skylar. "Except the power, that is. We're going to go next door to see what's happening."

"We'll join you," said Phil.

A few minutes later they headed out. Along the way, the group cleared debris from the porch and walkway. Ezzy helped Luke move a big palm frond aside, surprised at how heavy it was. She noticed a lot of leaves and twigs floating in the canal beside the dock. None of the boats appeared damaged. A small pile of seaweed suggested that during the storm the ocean had risen and flowed over the dock.

Upon entering Aquarius Station headquarters, Ezzy noticed that inside, it was unusually dark, warm, and eerily quiet.

"Hellooooo!" said Gracie. "Anyone here?"

"Hang on a second," yelled a voice from outside.

Ezzy heard a motor start up. A few lights came on and she felt a whoosh of cool air. "Hey, did the power just come on?"

Otter stepped through the sliding glass doors. "Nope, sorry to say, just our backup generator."

"Everything okay otherwise?" Dr. Skylar asked.

"Minor damage around. Downed trees probably took out some power lines and there's some flooding."

"How long do you think the power will be out?" asked Phil.

"Hard to say," answered Otter. "Around here it can take a while. You guys are welcome to hang out here if you'd like."

"What about the underwater lab?" asked Luke.

"We're sending a team out shortly to check on it," replied Otter as his cell phone rang. He took it from his short's pocket. "Otter here. What? Sorry, our team is headed out to check on the station. We don't have anyone to spare right now. No, I'm afraid Alec is not available at the moment."

Otter frowned as he pocketed the phone.

"What's happening?" asked Phil.

"Is everything okay?" added Gracie.

Otter shook his head. "It's the fish farm. Their power is out too, and they only have enough generator power to chill the water in their breed stock tanks and a few of the grow out pools. If the power doesn't come back on soon, the ornamental fish probably won't make it."

"Is there anything we can do to help?" asked Dr. Skylar.

"Yeah," said Luke.

"That was Justin calling. He's looking for some help to manually cool the water. But I can't spare any of the staff right now."

"Manually cool the water?" said Ezzy. "What does that mean?"

"Carting in ice and dumping it in to keep the water at the right temperature."

"We could help with that," offered Gracie.

"Yeah. Us too," added Luke. "Right, Dad?"

"Sure," said his father.

"Great," responded Otter. "I'll call Justin back and let him know. We've got an ice machine downstairs. The ice probably stayed frozen overnight. Why don't you fill a couple coolers and bring some over."

"On it," said Gracie, racing out the door.

Before following, Phil turned to the others. "Come on. We've got that rental car. We'll put the coolers in there and head over."

"Yay," said Luke. "We can help save the fish." He turned to Ezzy with a smirk. "And help Justin out."

Ezzy blushed. "That's cool." She was excited about helping Justin (and the fish) and wondered if Dr. Mudbourne would be in his lab studying the half-a-giant-lionfish they'd retrieved the day before.

*   *   *

The group arrived at the fish farm with three large coolers filled with ice. Justin met them in the parking lot. His t-shirt was soaked with water and shorts stained. "Otter called and said you were on your way over with some ice. Thanks. We need to keep the water cool in the ornamental fish tanks until the power comes back on or until we can get a couple more generators."

Ezzy thought he looked kinda stressed out. It made

her appreciate Justin even more. He wasn't confident and smiling all the time. He was more like her.

"Where's the rest of the staff?" asked Dr. Skylar.

Justin sighed. "We don't actually have a lot of people. And the folks who work here are mostly at home dealing with their own issues. Come on. There's a couple wheelbarrows near the dock we can use to move the coolers." He led them to the boat ramp and dock beside the canal connected to Florida Bay. Tied up beside the dock was the fish farm's boat.

"Hey, check it out," said Justin, pointing to the water. "Two manatees."

Ezzy and Luke ran onto the dock. But as Ezzy stepped onto the aging wood, her foot nicked the edge of a slightly raised board. She stumbled. To break her fall, Ezzy grabbed for what was closest. It was hanging on a post nearby—an orange ring buoy and line.

Hanging by the ring buoy, she twisted around and sheepishly said to the others, "Glad this was here."

Her father went to her side. "You okay?"

As she stood up, Ezzy felt her face turning red. "Yeah."

"Guess it was a real *lifesaver*," he added.

Ezzy shook her head at her dad and herself. She stepped closer to the canal, looking intently at the water while trying to hide her embarrassment. The water was shallow and clear, and near the bottom lounged two rotund gray bodies with small heads and large paddle-like tails. Ezzy leaned closer. She'd never seen a manatee in the wild.

"Whoa!" said Luke. "They're huge."

Ezzy smiled. Manatees weren't on her wild-things-that-could-kill-you list. She'd heard they were like gentle undersea cows. She'd even heard a story about someone who had been hugged by a manatee while snorkeling. The woman had said it was one of the best moments of her life.

"They're one of my favorites," exclaimed Gracie. "So cute."

"And big," added Dr. Skylar. "What's that white stripe on one's back?"

Justin frowned. "That's a propeller scar. Too many boaters don't watch out for them or slow down in manatee zones."

"That's terrible," groaned Luke.

Ezzy nodded, wondering who in the world wouldn't go a little slower for manatees.

One of the manatees rose slowly to the surface and poked a short, flattened snout out of the water. Ezzy heard a loud intake of air. The manatee ducked its small head under and descended back to the bottom. Soon, the water around the manatees turned cloudy.

"Must be eating the sea grass," said Justin. "It stirs up the mud. They come in here sometimes to feed. In some places the sea grass has died off because of pollution and algae blooms."

The other manatee rose slowly to the surface and

raised its entire head out of the water. Ezzy watched closely as it took a breath. Its flat muzzle was covered in thick whiskers. Behind that were two tiny round eyes. The manatee rolled over, putting its fat belly on show. It then touched a short gray flipper to its mouth.

Luke squealed with delight. "What's it doing?"

"I think it's saying feed me," Justin told him. "Some people feed them lettuce or give them freshwater with a hose. But you're not really supposed to do that."

"Even if there's not enough sea grass and they're hungry?" asked Luke.

"Well, it's a hard call," replied Justin. "We don't want to change their natural behavior. Luckily, they're okay here so far. Though we still have a problem with boaters going too fast and hitting them." He turned to look at the captain who was aboard the fish farm boat.

"Hey, don't look at me. I slow down for manatees."

"We'd better go," urged Justin. "The water in the fish tanks is warming up." He turned to the captain. "Just borrowing the wheelbarrows."

"Bring 'em back when you're done. Might need 'em in a bit."

Justin nodded as he pushed a wheelbarrow. Phil took hold of another. "Headed out, Captain?"

The man turned to Phil. "Uh... will probably go out to check on some gear in the Bay."

Ezzy noticed Justin give the captain a strange look and then shrug. As the others took the wheelbarrows to the car and began to load the coolers, Ezzy lagged behind to watch the captain, her suspicious nature kicking in. She was about to join the group, when out of the corner of her eye she sensed movement. She looked back and saw Dr. Mudbourne scurry to the boat. He handed the captain a bucket and looked around as if checking to see if anyone was watching. Ezzy quickly wheeled around, hoping he hadn't seen her and wondering what he was up to.

A few minutes later, Ezzy followed as the group entered the building housing the ornamental fish. Inside, it was warm and rapidly becoming stuffy. While the Smiths and Dr. Skylar unloaded the coolers and returned the wheelbarrows, Justin gave Ezzy and Luke digital laser thermometers. "The ideal temperature in the tanks is seventy to seventy-five degrees. If the water warms up too much more than that and stays that way, the fish won't last, especially the clownfish and tangs. You guys go around and measure the temperature. Just point the thermometer at the water and press this button. A temperature reading will come up. If you find any tank that is eighty degrees or higher, let me know and we'll dump in some ice."

Ezzy glanced around. There were at least thirty small raised rectangular tanks in the room.

The others returned and Justin gave them small glass laboratory jars. "We can use these for the ice. This amount should be enough to cool the water, but not dilute it too much. I also have some Instant Ocean we can add if the salt level or salinity gets too low. I'll measure that."

The team quickly got to work. Ezzy and Luke went to the tanks and began measuring the water temperature.

"Got one!" yelled Luke. "Eighty."

Gracie rushed over with some ice.

"Over here," shouted Ezzy. "Eighty-two."

Dr. Skylar ran to her with an ice-filled jar.

About forty-five minutes later, they'd checked and cooled down most of the tanks. Justin added some Instant Ocean to a few to keep the salinity at the right level.

"Nice work, everyone," said a new voice. Ezzy recognized it immediately. Dr. Mudbourne had just walked through the door that led up to his lab. "Justin told me you were coming over. Thank you for your help. I've got a couple more generators coming. They should be here soon."

"Phew," said Justin. "That's great news."

"Why don't you all take a break up in the lab," suggested the scientist. "With the generator on, there's air conditioning and you can get some water."

Ezzy peered at the man. He was being strangely nice and appeared somewhat disheveled. His white lab coat was wrinkled and stained, and deep creases marked the man's face.

"You must be Dr. Mudbourne," said Phil. "I'm Phil, and that gorgeous creature by the yellow tang tank is my wife, Gracie."

"Nice to meet you," said Gracie. "We'd love to come up to your lab if you think it's okay to leave these cuties in the tanks."

"No worries," said Dr. Mudbourne. "If the additional generators aren't here soon, you can always come back down. Besides, I want to show you what I discovered about the lionfish."

"You mean the big, creepy, lionfish," corrected Ezzy.

For just an instant, the scientist glared at her before waving them toward the door.

"It is hot in here," said Justin. "Maybe a short break would be good."

The group headed to the lab. On the way, Ezzy nudged Luke, nodded toward Dr. Mudbourne and whispered, "He's acting weird."

"Yeah," said Luke. "But don't you want to see what he found out about the big lionfish?"

She nodded, but she didn't trust the guy or his new-found caring personality.

* * *

History Repeats Itself

When they entered the lab, the first thing Ezzy noticed was how different it looked. Most of the equipment had been packed up or removed. She thought maybe it was because of the storm. Then she noticed the fish tanks along the far wall. They were the same as before and full of small fish.

Her father obviously noticed the difference too. "Did you pack up for the storm?" he asked.

"Like, dude," said Justin. "What's going on?"

"Unfortunately, or maybe fortunately," replied Dr. Mudbourne. "I did in fact confirm that the large lionfish are from my lab. It looks like our genetic modifications had a few side effects, like growing quickly and larger than normal."

"And getting meaner," Ezzy added.

Dr. Mudbourne shot her a look like he'd like to feed her to their sharks and groupers. "We can work on the side effects," he said. "And actually, if I can learn more, this discovery could be put to good use. We can try to alter our other stocks to grow bigger, faster. It will be a win-win for food production."

Luke raised his hand.

The scientist rolled his eyes and sighed. "Now what?"

"Uh, but what about the lionfish that are still out there?"

"That, my young man, is a bit of a problem."

"You can say that again," added Ezzy.

"And if someone catches those fish and does the work," Dr. Mudbourne added, "they'll discover that they've been genetically altered. And unless they're complete idiots—" The man paused and looked at Ezzy.

"Hey."

"—As I was saying," he continued, "unless they are dimwits, complete numbskulls, they'll figure out the connection to my lab."

"You should know," said Dr. Skylar, "we told Otter back at the Sea Station about the possible connection. And I believe he has already notified the Fish and Wildlife Service. And did you get my message? We were wondering if those big lionfish could have produced any offspring while they've been out there."

"Yeah," said Luke. "Like monster mutant babies."

Dr. Mudbourne shook his head. "No, I don't think they could have reproduced. We've been struggling to get them to spawn in the lab. It is one of the biggest challenges. We can make them sterile and not reproduce, but we cannot seem to get them to reproduce and pass on a sterile gene."

"Well, there's some good news," said Gracie.

The scientist stepped toward the door and stroked his chin as if deep in thought. "Now as for you talking to the authorities. I figured that might happen. Looks like I need to get rid of those fish before anyone else can confirm they came from my lab. Luckily, the Fish and Wildlife guys will have their hands full for a while with cleanup after the storm."

Ezzy noticed Phil staring suspiciously at the scientist before he asked. "What exactly are you planning to do?"

"I need to kill those fish and dispose of the bodies ASAP," said the scientist, reaching for the door. Before any of them could react, he snatched it open and slipped through. Phil leapt forward to prevent the door from closing all the way. But he was too late. Ezzy heard a loud click. Phil tried the handle. Locked. Dr. Mudbourne stared at them through the glass and Ezzy swore he mouthed *sorry* before walking out of sight.

"Oh no," exclaimed Luke. "Not this again."

Ezzy knew what he was thinking. It was like

Greenland all over again—when they got locked in a massage room in the unfinished spa building.

"Hang on," said Justin, stepping to the keypad beside the door. He punched the buttons. Nothing happened. "He must have changed the code. But I don't get what's going on. Why'd the dude lock us in?"

"I truly wanted to give the man the benefit of the doubt," said Dr. Skylar. "I did a little research on him. Dr. Mudbourne is a respected scientist, though he's made some questionable calls in the past when it comes to ethics, according to what I read. Sometimes, even people with good intentions do bad things."

"Right," said Phil. "If Mudbourne does away with the fish before anyone else catches one, including the authorities, they'll be no evidence linking them to his lab."

"Which would be bad for business or getting investors," added Gracie.

"But he already told us they came from the lab," said Ezzy. "Even if he does away with the big, creepy, lionfish, we know the truth and can tell people."

"It would be our word against his," said Dr. Skylar.

Gracie looked purposely around the room. "More likely, the man is planning to do away with the fish and then hightail it out of here. Probably move his operation somewhere else."

"And use what he discovered about the lionfish to grow fish bigger and faster," added Phil. "I think he locked us in here to buy some time."

"Well, on the bright side," noted Gracie. "At least he didn't try to get rid of us permanently."

Just then Ezzy smelled something almost sweet. It didn't smell like perfume or anything familiar. "Do you guys smell something?"

Luke nodded. "Uh huh."

"Everyone, cover your nose and mouths!" shouted Phil as he pulled his shirt up over his mouth and nose.

Dr. Skylar pulled his shirt up before helping Ezzy and Luke do the same.

Phil and Gracie searched the room.

"Over here!" said Gracie in a muffled voice. "Stay back. Mudbourne may not be trying to kill us... maybe... but I think he's attempting to drug us."

Ezzy stayed where she was but could see what Gracie had uncovered. Hidden behind a box was a glass flask sitting atop a lit Bunsen burner. A cloud of steam rose above a pinkish liquid in the flask.

Phil joined his wife and together they found the controls to the burner and turned it off. As Gracie reached for a nearby book to place atop the flask, she wobbled. Phil grabbed her but faltered. The two of them managed to get the book atop the flask before they both sank in a slow faint to the floor.

Ezzy rushed toward them, but her father grabbed her arm and held her back. "Hold on, Ez. Stay low and

I'll try to disperse whatever was coming out of that flask." As Ezzy crawled to the Smiths on the floor, her father grabbed a towel draped over a chair and waved it through the air above the Smiths. He then squatted down beside them. "I think they're just passed out."

Justin still stood by the keypad lock. A look of shock on his face. "I can't believe this."

"I can," said Luke through his shirt. "We've been in this situation before." He turned to Ezzy. "Remember how we escaped last time?"

Ezzy nodded and searched the ceiling. "There's one," she said pointing to a slotted square vent cover.

"I'm not sure what you're talking about," said Justin. "But I have an idea of my own." He picked up a nearby chair and tried to smash the glass door. It bounced off without leaving a dent. "It was worth a shot." He whipped out his cell phone. "I'm calling 911." He punched in the numbers and put the phone to his ear. "It's not going through. Must be because of the storm and too many people calling."

Dr. Skylar took out his phone and also tried 911. "Hello, I'd like to report an emergency." He paused listening. "Well, no, no one is seriously injured or dying. I think. But... okay, we'll try later."

He turned to the group and shook his head before punching in another number. "Otter, thank goodness you answered. We're locked in Mudbourne's lab. He tried to drug us." He again paused listening. "Yes, really. We think he's going out on their boat to get the

168 Ellen Prager • Escape Undersea

lionfish so no one will know the connection to the lab and locked us in to buy time. Okay, thanks."

"Otter's out on the boat but is going to call a couple people he knows with the authorities," Dr. Skylar told them. "But he isn't sure how soon they can get here. With the power out and flooding, they're busy. Like the other guy said, unless it's life or death, or a serious injury, they can't respond right away. We may be stuck in here a while."

"But we need to stop Mudbourne before he gets away," said Luke.

Ezzy pointed to the air conditioning vent. "Not sure you guys can fit, but Luke and I could climb out and try to find someone to help open the door."

Dr. Skylar was tending to the Smiths, who had started to come around. "I would rather we all stay together. I don't want you two going off on your own again."

"Come on, Dad," said Luke. "We did it before. No problem. We'll just go and find someone to help get you guys out of here."

"Hey," said Justin. "If you turn off the generator, maybe the door will unlock."

"Cool," said Ezzy, thinking this would be an opportunity to make up for her embarrassing stumble and all-around awkwardness. To showcase her courageous side. As long as she didn't think too much about what could go wrong. "We'll get out, Dad. Find the generator and turn it off. Then you guys can get out and join us."

She turned to Justin. "Where's the generator?"

"It's outside, near the end of the building on the Bay side," he replied.

"Got it," said Luke turning to his father. "Can we do it?"

The Smiths sat up, but still looked dazed and a bit woozy.

Dr. Skylar hesitated. "Okay, but be careful and don't take any risks. You can always come back, and we can wait it out."

"Excellent," said Ezzy, feeling a purpose and pride that amped up her courage. And because she and Luke had done it before, she was confident they could escape through the vent shaft. She strode to a spot directly below the vent. "First we need to get up there and then we need to pry off the cover."

Justin pushed a table toward Ezzy. "I bet with a chair on top of this table you could reach. I'll try to find a screwdriver or something."

"How about this?" said Luke with a grin, holding up his swiss army knife. "It worked before."

"Perfect," said Ezzy. "Can someone hold the chair while I climb up." She looked hopefully toward Justin.

"Got it," he said, reaching for a chair.

"Hang on," said Dr. Skylar who'd left the Smiths sitting on the floor. He strode to Ezzy and the table. "You don't have to do this all by yourself this time. I'll climb up, get the vent cover off and help you up."

"Thanks, Dad," said Ezzy, glad her father was with them this time.

Dr. Skylar jumped up onto the table and Luke passed him the swiss army knife. He stood up and reached for the vent cover. After a little fiddling, he announced, "Got it."

"Okay, Ez and Luke," he said. "You're up."

Ezzy climbed onto the table.

"Ready?" her father asked.

"Ready."

He lifted her to the vent opening and whispered, "Mom would be proud."

Ezzy grinned as a wave of strength flowed through her body. Her father lifted her higher and she reached up and into the vent shaft.

"If you need to, stand on my shoulders," he told her.

Ezzy wiggled her feet onto her father's shoulders and stood up. "I'm gonna jump."

"Go for it," he said.

Ezzy pushed off and pulled herself into the square ventilation shaft. It brought back memories. "We can do this," she said quietly. She maneuvered around inside the shaft so that she was looking down. "Your turn, Luke."

Justin helped Luke climb onto the table and his father lifted him up. "Just like Ez, stand on my shoulders."

Luke reached up to Ezzy's outstretched hands and stood on his father's shoulders.

"When I say three," said Ezzy. "Jump."

Luke nodded.

"One. Two. Three... jump!"

Luke pushed off his father's shoulders as Ezzy pulled him up. He landed on his stomach with his legs swinging out below the vent shaft. "Ooph!"

Ezzy pulled him in and then looked down at her father and the others. "Okay. We're good to go."

"Hang on," said her dad. "Do you have your phone with you?"

Ezzy shook her head. "It was low on charge so I left it at the base."

"Okay, take mine," he said. "I'll use the tracking device and someone else's phone to follow you."

Phil and Gracie Smith were now standing. "We can use mine," offered Phil. "Besides, you have my number in your phone. So Ezzy, you can call or text if there's a problem or as soon as you get out."

Dr. Skylar tossed his phone up to Ezzy, who caught it on the first try. "Got it."

"See ya later, alligator," Luke said to his father.

"After a while, not a crocodile."

"Good luck," said Justin.

Ezzy grinned and said to Luke. "Let's do this."

The two of them got onto their hands and knees.

Ezzy took the lead crawling down the vent shaft. They headed into a rush of cool air.

"Brrr!" said Luke.

"Feels great," countered Ezzy.

The two of them scrambled down the shaft. Soon they came to an intersection.

"I think the ornamental fish tanks are that way," she said pointing left. She peered down the shaft in that direction. Dead end. "Looks like we go straight."

She continued crawling with Luke following close behind.

A few minutes later, Luke tapped her foot. "Do you hear something?"

Ezzy stopped and stayed still. An unfamiliar noise echoed through the ventilation shaft. Ahead, a bend to the right blocked the view. She crawled around the bend and froze. About forty feet ahead was the source of the noise—a large rotating fan. "Uh oh."

Luke wiggled up beside her. "How do we get past *that?*"

Ezzy decided to get a closer look to see if there was some way around the fan's revolving blades. She was so focused on the fan, Ezzy nearly fell into a vertical shaft about fifteen feet in front of the fan. "Yikes!"

"What?" Luke called out.

"I think there's a way out right here."

Luke scrambled up beside her and the two of them peered down the short shaft. A slotted vent cover blocked the view. Ezzy looked closer. What she could see through the narrow openings didn't look right. "There's something moving down there."

"I think it's water," said Luke. "Maybe it's one of the fish tanks."

"Maybe," said Ezzy. "I'll try to kick the cover off."

Ezzy sat on the edge of the vertical shaft and kicked downward as hard as she could. The slotted cover shook but didn't come loose. She kicked again and one edge broke free. "One more should do it." She kicked and the cover flew off. Ezzy heard a splash and some loud swishing sounds. She and Luke leaned down into the shaft to see what lay below.

It's definitely water, thought Ezzy. And then she saw a fin.

*   *   *

Sharks in the Pool

E zzy and Luke leaned further down into the short vertical shaft.

"It's a tank," Luke observed. "Looks like there's fish in it."

"Yeah, fish all right," moaned Ezzy. "Sharks."

Another fin sliced through the water below.

"It must be the tank they're using to try to teach sharks and groupers to eat lionfish," Luke offered. "Don't see any groupers, though."

"Just sharks."

"Looks like two of them. Can't tell what kind."

"Does it really matter?" said Ezzy. "They're sharks."

"Yeah, and remember what Justin said. They keep them hungry, so they'll eat the lionfish."

"You had to remind me," groaned Ezzy, as her heart pounded, and her stomach began doing flip flops.

"At least the water will make the landing easier this time," said Luke.

"Forget the landing," said Ezzy. "They're sharks. You know, sharp teeth, biting, feeding frenzy, lots of blood, that sort of thing."

"Ez, sharks don't really eat people, most of the time."

"Most of the time," Ezzy repeated. "Yeah, but they could still take a nibble."

"What if we jump in at the same time?" Luke suggested. "It might scare them and give us time to get out."

"Or make them mad."

"Do you have a better idea?" Luke asked.

"Maybe we should go back and wait it out. Like Dad said. Eventually someone will come and let us out of the lab."

Luke shook his head. "No. We need to get everyone out and stop Mudbourne from getting rid of all the lionfish. It's the only evidence connecting those fish to his lab."

Ezzy's heart thumped so hard she was surprised Luke couldn't hear it. Sharks had always been one of her greatest fears. Otter and others kept telling her they weren't vicious people eaters. The question was—was she willing to test that theory out? She really wanted to jump and help the others get out of the lab, and stop Mudbourne, but she *really*, really did not want to jump into a tank of sharks.

"I could do it, Ez," Luke told her. "And go turn off the generator. We don't both have to go."

Ezzy took a deep breath. She wasn't about to let her little brother do it alone. That would be bad on so many levels. This would be the biggest test so far of the new braver, more adventurous Ezzy. She took a deep breath and said firmly, "No, we'll do it together."

"Ready?" Luke asked.

"No," answered Ezzy. "Give me a minute to consider what might be my last moments on Earth."

Luke rolled his eyes. "People are not good shark food, Ez. Let's go on three."

Ezzy shook her hands and rolled her neck around trying to loosen up. She remembered that if she thought too much about stuff her fear got worse. She nodded. "Okay. We'll go on three."

"Ready," said Luke.

"One... two... two and a half... two and three-quarters."

"Three!" Luke yelled and jumped.

Ezzy closed her eyes and leapt out of the shaft. The fall was quick. Before she knew it, Ezzy was in the water. She hit the bottom of the tank and pushed off.

Immediately, she started to kick and pull as if it was the race of her life, make that for her life. Just as Ezzy's hand hit the side of the tank, something bumped her leg. She nearly flew out of the water, over the rim of the tank, and fell to the floor. Dripping wet, Ezzy rolled onto her back and glanced at her leg. No blood. She'd made it. Ezzy sprang to her feet. "Luke?"

"Over here," he responded from the other side of the tank.

Ezzy ran to him. "You okay?"

Luke was sitting on the floor, soaking wet with a hand on his head. "You'll never believe what happened. I ran right into one of the sharks. We bumped heads. I'm not sure which of us was more surprised."

"Let me see," Ezzy said, expecting to see blood and teeth marks.

Luke pulled his hand away. A bump was swelling up with a small scrape atop it.

"Dad will want to take a look at that," said Ezzy.

As soon as she mentioned her father, Ezzy remembered his phone. She reached into her pocket. "Oops."

"What?" asked Luke.

Ezzy peered into the tank. "Dad's phone. Must have fallen out when we jumped in."

"Come on," said Luke. "We can get the phone later."

"Or not," said Ezzy.

The two of them raced for the door. As Ezzy ran

by another above-ground tank she peeked inside. A couple of three-foot-long groupers hovered in the water looking up at her. *Why couldn't that have been the tank under the vent shaft?*

Once outside, Ezzy and Luke stopped to get their bearings.

Ezzy swiveled around looking for water. "Justin said the generator is on the side of the building near the Bay."

"There," said Luke pointing to a patch of greenish water visible through some mangroves.

They ran along the side of the building toward the Bay. At the far end, they turned right. Ezzy heard a motor running. She and Luke ran toward the noise. It led them to a big, yellow, vibrating, metal box. "Look for the off switch," Ezzy told him.

Luke pointed to a red button labeled STOP. Ezzy nodded and he pushed it. The generator immediately shut off.

"That should do it," said Ezzy. "Let's go."

They turned, ready to run back around the building, when the sound of a motorboat cruising nearby caught Ezzy's attention. She ran to the mangroves lining the shore. Luke followed. Through the tangle of orangey-red branch-like roots, Ezzy caught a glimpse of a boat. It looked like the fish farm boat. She wondered if Dr. Mudbourne was on it. Staying low so as not to be seen, she climbed out onto the mangrove's thick roots for a better view.

"It's Mudbourne," she whispered. "On the fish farm boat."

"What's he doing?"

"Looks like they're headed for the canal by the dock."

"Let's go find Dad and the others," Luke suggested.

"You go," said Ezzy. "I'm going to see what they're doing. I'll stay out of sight. Find the others and meet me over by the dock."

Luke nodded and took off.

Ezzy carefully climbed off the mangrove roots. Staying low and behind the vegetation, she crept along the shore until she came to a small shed. Silently, she made her way around it to the far corner. There, Ezzy leaned past the shed just enough to see the dock. The fish farm boat was entering the canal with Dr. Mudbourne sitting at the stern. He appeared to be drizzling something into the water behind the boat as it headed for the dock.

It sounded to Ezzy like Dr. Mudbourne and the captain were talking, but from behind the shed she couldn't tell what they were saying. Ezzy wanted to get closer but was afraid of being seen. *I just jumped into a tank of sharks,* she said to herself. *I can do this.* Balling her fists, Ezzy nodded to herself and slipped out from behind the building. Staying low, she ran to a clump of mangroves beside the dock and dove to the ground behind them.

"With the trail of pheromones in the water, the fish should track here soon."

"Are you sure it's going to work, Mudbourne?"

"Yes."

Ezzy's eyes widened in realization. Dr. Mudbourne was using his lionfish love potion to lure the fish into the canal beside the dock. She wondered what they were going to do once the giant lionfish arrived. Ezzy quietly swiveled around searching for the group that had been trapped in the lab, hoping they would arrive soon. She heard the boat nudge against the dock and turned back to watch.

Dr. Mudbourne stepped off the boat onto the dock while speaking to the captain. "Keep an eye out for those fish. Let me know if you see them, and if needed, herd them into the canal."

"Got it," the captain replied, before walking to the rail and handing something to the scientist. "You're going to need these dealing with that stuff."

"Right," said the scientist.

Ezzy cautiously stuck her head through the mangroves to get a closer look at what the captain had given Mudbourne. It looked like a pair of gloves and a mask. It made Ezzy think of the pandemic. *What were they planning?*

* * *

Luke and the Lionfish

The fish farm boat pulled slowly away from the dock, heading back into Florida Bay. Ezzy ducked lower behind the mangroves, inched closer, and watched Dr. Mudbourne. The man glanced around and then walked toward the shed she'd been hiding behind before. He put on the gloves and mask the captain had given him and went inside. Worried he might see her on the way back to the dock, Ezzy crept into the mangroves and squatted down, teetering on the branch-like roots. She found a handhold to steady herself, but it was hard to stay low and balanced on the roots. And inside the mangroves the heat went from medium-high to sauna. Sweat began to trickle down Ezzy's face and slicken her hands.

Dr. Mudbourne exited the shed carrying a plastic jug and was no longer wearing the gloves and mask. As he neared where she was hiding, Ezzy held her breath. But slick with sweat, her hands slipped. She grabbed onto another branch to prevent falling. The whole bush shook. Ezzy prayed the man wouldn't notice as he walked by.

Dr. Mudbourne strode past her hiding spot, and Ezzy let out a long sigh before climbing out of the mangroves. She crawled back to where she'd hidden before and lay on the ground. The scientist placed the jug on the dock before taking a phone from his pocket. "Any sign of the fish? How far out? Okay, ready here."

The man walked along the dock toward Florida Bay, staring out into the water beyond the canal. Ezzy inched closer to the jug to see if there was a label or something that would reveal what it contained. She heard a loud intake of air from the canal. Recognizing the sound, Ezzy crept even closer to get a view of the water. A manatee had surfaced to breathe.

"You!"

Ezzy tried to scramble away, but the scientist was too fast. He grabbed her arm and hauled her up.

"I thought I'd taken you and your nosy group out of the equation for at least a little while. But here you are."

"Let go," shouted Ezzy.

Dr. Mudbourne dragged her across the dock.

"My father and the others will be here any

minute!"

The man looked around. "Then I better get things done quickly."

Ezzy tried to squirm out of his grasp and scream, but he held her tight and put a hand over her mouth. The scientist dragged her toward the edge of the dock. "The fish must be close now."

"Ezzy!" someone shouted.

Ezzy stomped on the scientist's foot but still he held on. As he wheeled her around, Ezzy saw her father, Luke, and the Smiths racing toward them.

"Dad!" she tried to shout.

"Hold it right there," warned Dr. Mudbourne taking his hand from Ezzy's mouth and whispering to her, "Stay still and be quiet."

The group stopped.

"The lionfish are headed into the canal," said Dr. Mudbourne. "If you come any closer, your lovely little girl here will be going for a swim to join them."

"Don't do anything rash," urged Dr. Skylar.

Phil Smith held up a partially torn label. "We know what you're planning, Mudbourne. We found this in the lab."

"You wanted me to kill the lionfish," he replied. "That's just what I'm doing."

Luke stepped forward, but his father grabbed his arm to hold him back. "No. Luke, stay here." He turned to Dr. Mudbourne. "But if you do it, you'll kill everything in the water."

Ezzy looked at the others confused.

"The jug by his feet, Ez," said her father. "It's poison. He's going to dump it into the canal."

"Very good," said the scientist. "But now I have a problem. I can't keep hold of the girl and dump it in. And the lionfish should be here any minute."

Ezzy glanced into the water and croaked, "What about the manatees?"

"Sorry," said the scientist. "It can't be helped. I would prefer not to kill them. But I guess it's what you call collateral damage." He turned to the group. "Send the boy over. The rest of you stay exactly where you are. Try anything and I'll dump the girl into the canal. If the lionfish don't get her, the poison will."

Dr. Skylar grimaced and seemed about to lunge forward. Phil put a hand on his arm and whispered something in his ear.

"Don't try anything," said Dr. Mudbourne. "It's not worth it. I'm just going to do away with the evidence and then I'll be out of here. No one has to get hurt. Now send the boy over. He can do the pouring for me."

Ezzy shook her head. "No. Leave him out of this."

"Concern for your little brother," said Dr. Mudbourne. "How sweet. Okay, son, walk over here slowly." He kept hold of Ezzy and his eyes on the others.

Luke nodded to his father. "It's okay, Dad. I can do this."

Ezzy watched Luke carefully. She recognized the look on his face. Like in the Galápagos Islands when he acted all weird to scare away the animals so the poachers couldn't get them or when he tripped to frighten the iguana away. Her little brother was ready for mischief and planning something.

Luke walked slowly to the dock. He had a kind of goofy expression on his face. It was the I'm-just-a-little-kid-don't-worry-about-me look. He reached the dock and whimpered, "Don't hurt me."

Dr. Mudbourne smiled. "Don't worry little man. Nothing will happen to you or your sister as long as you do what I say. I'm really not a *bad* guy."

Ezzy glared at the man and then heard another intake of air from the water. Luke must have heard it too. They both turned and watched as the cute whiskered snout of another manatee rose out of the water.

Ezzy saw Luke's expression change. His eyes narrowed and lips puckered. He was getting ready to do something. Ezzy didn't know what, but figured she better be ready for anything.

From outside the canal, a boat's horn blasted. Ezzy squirmed and the scientist tightened his grip.

"Okay boy," said Dr. Mudbourne. "The lionfish are heading into the canal. Unscrew the cap on that jug. Once they're near the dock, pour it into the water."

"Okay," he said meekly.

Oh boy, thought Ezzy. He's been taking lessons from the Smiths and is really playing it up.

Another blast of the horn rang out. Splashing at the entrance to the canal drew everyone's attention. Ezzy saw the dorsal spines of several giant lionfish sticking out of the water as they headed in.

"My plan is working perfectly," announced Dr. Mudbourne before looking at Luke. "Get ready, kid."

Luke nodded before slyly winking at Ezzy. Here we go, she thought, tensing.

Luke took a step toward the jug as if following the scientist's orders. He glanced down and Ezzy noticed what lay in his path. Luke's toe hit the raised board she'd tripped over earlier. He stumbled forward, knocking the jug toward the scientist. The man reacted on instinct and reared back. Ezzy stomped on his foot and pushed him away with all her might. Mudbourne teetered on the edge of the dock and began to fall, but he still had hold of Ezzy's arm. As he fell into the water, Dr. Mudbourne pulled Ezzy in with him.

"No!" shouted Luke.

To Ezzy, it seemed to happen in slow motion. As soon as Mudbourne began to fall, she knew she was in trouble. She couldn't shake his grasp. Her feet slipped off the dock and she steeled herself, glancing back at Luke. All at once she saw fear, shock, and guilt.

Ezzy hit the water and went under on top of the scientist. Nearly simultaneously, the water around her erupted. Bodies bumped; water splashed. Something struck her arm. Oh no, the lionfish, Ezzy thought. She hit the surface spluttering as something else, something hard, hit her head.

"Grab it!" someone yelled.

Just inches from Ezzy's face floated the orange ring buoy. She grabbed it. Instantly she began to move, gliding across the water. Behind her, Mudbourne rose to the surface and grabbed for Ezzy's foot. But she was already out of reach. Clinging to the ring buoy, Ezzy was pulled toward shore. Water splashed in her face, making it hard to see. As soon as Ezzy reached the boat ramp, she was helped out of the water and hauled to her feet.

A scream echoed across the canal. Ezzy whipped around. The lionfish now surrounded Dr. Mudbourne. They swirled about and bumped him as the water in the canal turned murky brown.

"Help," he shouted in a weakening voice. "Help me."

Dr. Skylar ran to Ezzy's side on the boat ramp. "Come on, swim for it," he yelled to the man.

Standing beside Ezzy were Justin and Alec. The two of them held the ring buoy and attached line in their hands. Justin tossed the buoy out to Dr. Mudbourne.

"Grab it," Justin yelled again.

But the scientist had disappeared beneath the circling lionfish. Justin slowly pulled the ring buoy in. "That's no way to go even for him."

As the group gathered around Ezzy, they stared in silence at the giant fish in the canal. There was no sign of Dr. Mudbourne.

"Where'd he go?" asked Luke.

"Is he dead?" asked Ezzy. "Like really dead?"

"He had to have been stabbed numerous times by all the lionfish in there," said Dr. Skylar. "I don't see how he'd survive the toxins."

"Must have sunk to the bottom," added Phil.

"Shouldn't we do something?" asked Gracie.

"Do you want to go in there with those fish?" her husband responded.

She shook her head sadly. "Sorry, but nope."

"Maybe he swam out," suggested Luke.

Phil shook his head while saying, "Maybe."

"What's more important," said Dr. Skylar to Ezzy, "is that you're safe." He pulled her into a tight hug.

"Yeah," said Luke joining the hug.

"Yeah," said the Smiths, piling onto the others.

Dr. Skylar turned to Justin and Alec. "Thank god you two showed up when you did."

Justin nodded. "I got a call from Alec's mother while I was checking on the fish tanks after we got out of the lab. She said she was bringing him over to help and asked if I could meet him in the parking lot."

Alec looked at them and nodded. "I wanted to help the fish."

"After his mother dropped him off and left," said Justin. "We heard someone shouting. So, we ran to the boat ramp." He turned to Ezzy. "That's when we saw you fall in. I guess my training kicked in and I threw the ring buoy. Alec helped me pull you in."

"You guys saved me," said Ezzy. Without thinking she hugged Justin. When she realized what she was doing, she turned red and quickly released him, stepping back. "Uh... thanks."

"Happy to help," said Justin. "Alec helped too."

Ezzy wanted to give Alec a hug too but wasn't sure if she should. To her surprise, he jumped forward and hugged her. "I'm glad we saved you."

"And I'm sorry I almost got you killed," Luke muttered.

"No," said Ezzy. "It's not your fault. That guy was nuts, and I didn't want you to dump in the poison." Ezzy looked to the water. The lionfish were heading out of the canal and there was still no sign of Dr. Mudbourne. "Hey, what happened to the manatees?"

"When you fell in it startled them," Luke told her. "Man, those manatees can move fast when they want to."

"It's their tails, dude," said Justin. "Like giant paddles."

"Anyway," said Luke. "The manatees hightailed it out of there."

"That must have been what made the water go all crazy when we fell in," said Ezzy. "I thought it was the lionfish."

"Nope," said Dr. Skylar. "Like Luke said, it was the

manatees. And when they headed out, I think they came face to face with the lionfish. But they didn't bother each other. So, the manatees went out and the lionfish swam in. I think it delayed the lionfish just enough so Justin and Alec here could pull you out."

"We'd better call 911 again," said Dr. Skylar. "Let them know what's happened. Have my phone, Ez?"

"Uh... well," she stuttered. "It kinda fell into a tank of sharks."

"Whaat?"

*   *   *

Disappeared

A bout an hour later, the power came back on. Shortly after, the police and a man from the Fish and Wildlife Service arrived at the fish farm. The group met them in the parking lot and explained what had happened.

"So where is Dr. Mudbourne now?" a policewoman asked.

"We're not sure," answered Dr. Skylar.

"What do you mean?"

"He's either dead," said Luke. "Or undead, just like his lionfish."

Ezzy rolled her eyes. "We think he's dead, but he kinda disappeared."

"Could he have swum out into Florida Bay?" asked Sam from the Fish and Wildlife Service.

"I guess. Maybe," said Justin. "The fish farm's boat never came back either."

"But," said Dr. Skylar. "Dr. Mudbourne must have been stabbed multiple times by the lionfish spines. With the size of those fish, I don't think anyone could have survived it."

"Unless they had anti-venom," Justin offered.

"What?" said Phil.

"Just sayin'," he replied. "That dude turned out to be kinda bad, but he *was* brilliant. If he thought he might encounter the lionfish while trying to catch or kill them, he might have prepared an anti-venom to their toxin. He could have cooked it up in the lab last night."

"He hardly had any time," said Gracie. "It seems unlikely. I'm sorry to say, I think he sank to the bottom and drifted out with the fish."

"And she's usually the one to look on the bright side," noted Phil.

"Well, we'll put a team in the water to look for the man," said the policewoman. "Keep an eye out for the boat. Let us know if it returns."

"What about the big, creepy lionfish?" asked Ezzy. "They're still some out there."

Sam nodded to her. "We have a special team that has been working to control the invasive lionfish population. I'll get them on it and see if we can find any more of the chemicals in Dr. Mudbourne's lab that he used to attract the lionfish. Besides, that could be a game-changer for us in trying to eradicate these fish."

Addressing the group, the policewoman added, "We'd appreciate it if you'd all stick around for a few days in case we have any additional questions."

They all agreed. Justin took Sam and the police-woman to Dr. Mudbourne's lab. Before he left, Ezzy thanked him again for saving her. The smile he gave in return was like a Christmas present in summer.

A car then sped into the parking lot and screeched to a halt. Otter jumped out and ran to the group. He grabbed Alec and wrapped his arms around the boy. "You okay?"

Alec nodded.

"More than okay," said Ezzy. "He helped save me."

Otter released his son. "That's my boy. When I heard what happened, I came right over. Everyone else okay too?"

The group assured him they were fine and then again recounted what had happened. Otter stood for several minutes shaking his head. "Who would ever have imagined."

"As I said before," noted Dr. Skylar. "Dr. Mudbourne wasn't all bad. His work was for good purposes, trying to curb the lionfish invasion and produce fish to help feed people."

"Until he visited nutzo-town," added Ezzy.

"What's going to happen to the fish farm and all the fish?" Luke asked.

"Not sure," answered Otter.

"Well, looks like we're sticking around for a few days," said Phil. "How about we commence mission poop tracker to see if any of that resort's wastewater is coming out on the reefs?"

Luke snickered.

"Poop tracker?" said Gracie. "You couldn't come up with a better name?"

"Crap Chaser? Feces Follower?"

"Poop Tracker it is," chuckled Gracie.

The others laughed.

"I've got an idea," said Otter turning to Dr. Skylar. "The sea station didn't sustain any real damage in the storm. Since you didn't get to make the visit with your kids, if your sinus infection has cleared up, how about a quick dive and tour tomorrow?"

"Can we go too?" asked Luke.

"What about the lionfish?" said Ezzy.

"Sure," replied Otter. "You two are welcome, of course. And hopefully the lionfish team will get those mutant versions. I doubt they'll show up at the station during the day anyway, especially with Gertrude and Gandolf hanging around. But we'll keep an eye out, just in case."

"Can Professor Miller go with you and put that dye sensor on the deep reef?" asked Gracie.

"Sure thing," said Otter. "We can do both tomorrow."

"Let the mission begin," said Phil. "Poop tracker's a go."

"Can we check on the fish before we leave?" asked Luke.

"Sure," said Dr. Skylar.

The group headed to the building housing the ornamental fish. With the power back on the air inside was already cooling down. They spent a few minutes talking with Justin, who was checking the water temperature in the tanks. Thankfully all the fish had survived. Alec pleaded with his father to stay and help Justin. Otter agreed, before leaving with the others to return to headquarters. After a busy and eventful morning, everyone took the rest of the day off to rest, eat, and prepare for the dive in the morning and the start of mission poop tracker.

*   *   *

Return to the Sea

The next morning there wasn't even the hint of a breeze. The sea was so calm it shimmered like glass. Ezzy never imagined the ocean could be so flat and still. The Skylars were aboard the Aquarius Sea Station boat, which was tied up to the mooring buoy above the undersea lab. The Smiths had stayed ashore to prepare for their visit to the resort later.

"Okay, everyone ready?" Otter asked.

Luke nodded.

Ezzy had tossed and turned the night before worrying about the dive. She raised her hand. "Uh, what about the lionfish? Any sign of them?"

"Our guys were diving all day yesterday and this morning," responded Otter. "There's been no sign of them."

"If you want to stay on the boat, Ez," her father said. "That's cool."

"Come on, sis," said Luke. "Gertrude and Gandolf are down there. They'll protect us if those monsters show up."

"Hopefully," muttered Ezzy.

"We're just going to pop down and go inside for a quick visit," said Otter. "So your dad can see the lab. Drew is already inside and everything's all set."

Ezzy didn't want to be left behind or seem like a wimp. "I'll go."

Lola, who was also aboard, helped Ezzy into her BC and tank. "I'm gonna swim down with you guys too. Don't worry."

Ezzy nodded, but her legs felt rubbery. She stared at the ocean's glassy surface. *Conditions couldn't be much better,* she said to herself. *I jumped into a pool of sharks. Compared to that, this is nothing.* Ezzy put her fins and mask on. She walked to the stern as her father and brother did giant strides into the water. Lola checked her tank. "You're good to go. Did you put a little air in your BC?"

Ezzy tapped her automatic inflator. She put her regulator into her mouth and took a test breath. Air flowed freely. Luke and her father floated at the surface watching as she stepped off the dive platform into the cool water.

Popping up to the surface, Ezzy felt refreshed. She peered into the water below and around her. No giant mutant lionfish. She kicked over to Luke and her father. Otter and Lola joined them.

"Everyone okay?" asked Otter.

They each gave him the okay sign.

"Let's head down," he said. "We'll take the scenic route to the station."

Ezzy took another breath from her regulator, exhaled slowly, and stared downward. The visibility was incredible. She could see the white sand bottom and patch reefs some thirty feet down. It was as if she was looking through glass or staring into a gigantic aquarium. Swiveling around, she again saw no sign of the creepy giant lionfish.

Letting some air out of her BC, Ezzy began to descend next to Luke and her father. Otter drifted down below her, and Lola hovered nearby. Ezzy glanced at her dive computer. She had plenty of air and was at fifteen feet. She continued deeper, pinching her nose and blowing out to clear her ears. Soon Ezzy could see schools of multicolored fish hovering over the reefs and swimming in and out of its crevasses. Three silver fish with dark blue stripes raced by. Except for the sound of her breathing, it was amazingly quiet, and there were still no giant lionfish anywhere in sight. She began to relax.

As Ezzy neared the reefs, she noticed a cluster of brown coral sticking up like antlers. On another was a small forest of purple sea fans. And beneath an overhang of platy brown coral hovered a tightly packed school of yellow-striped fish. Soon, Ezzy felt a calmness wash over her. Her worries and fears seem to disappear, as if dissolved in the surrounding sea.

Nearing the bottom, Ezzy adjusted the air in her BC to stop her descent and float, neutrally buoyant.

Otter gave each of them the okay sign and they returned it. He then kicked slowly ahead and waved the group forward, heading down a chute of sand between two ridge-like reefs. Ezzy followed. To her left she saw two small yellowish fish with black stripes and a big black spot near their tail. The butterflyfish were chasing each other around mounds of purple finger coral. The long pointy antennae of a spiny lobster poked out from a hole. She turned to the reef on her right. A large silver snapper stared back.

Ahead of Ezzy, Luke stopped, and she nearly swam into him. Gazing past her brother, Ezzy saw Otter pointing to a large hole in the reef to their right. He pointed to himself and the hole, indicating he was going to swim through. He again gave each of them the okay sign questioningly. Luke nodded excitedly before returning the okay sign as did her father. Ezzy put her finger to her thumb and nodded as well.

Ezzy watched as Otter swam toward the hole. It hardly looked big enough for him to fit through but soon his body and then fins disappeared inside. She watched as Luke went next, swimming through and out of sight. Her father indicated she should go next. Ezzy kicked gently and headed toward the hole, realizing she wasn't even nervous. She loved swimming underwater, in and around the coral reefs. It was a whole other world with so much to see and a peacefulness she rarely felt on land.

As Ezzy neared the hole, she could see it was the entrance to a tunnel under the reef. Without even pausing, she swam in. It was dim inside, but rays of light shining through holes overhead lit up the sandy bottom like spotlights on a stage. A cloud of small silver fish sparkled in front of her. Ezzy stared in wonder as they parted in graceful synchrony as she passed through. She turned over to look up. Her exhalation bubbles bounced on the ceiling of the tunnel, the underside of the reef. The silvery bubbles moved amid patches of bright orange and yellow sponge. She turned back over. Sticking out into the tunnel was a beautiful iridescent sponge that resembled a delicate purple vase. Up ahead, she saw Luke's fins disappear around a corner.

Ezzy kicked slowly and carefully so as not to disturb the sand. She turned left, following her brother. About fifteen feet away it got lighter. It was the tunnel's exit. Luke passed through and disappeared. Otter peeked in and waved to her. She waved back.

Making sure not to hit the reef around her, Ezzy swam carefully out of the tunnel. As she exited, something moved to her right, drawing her attention. She saw a flash of red and white stripes and swooshing frilly spines. Her heart leapt. Ezzy kicked hard speeding away. She caught up to Luke who was hanging in the water pointing to the tunnel entrance. She stopped and looked back. A small lionfish, only about six inches long, hovered near the reef. Ezzy breathed a sigh of relief. It wasn't a giant genetically altered lionfish, only one of the regular invasive species. Her father swam out of the tunnel. Taking his regulator from his mouth, he grinned at her and Luke.

From there it was a short swim to the Aquarius Sea Station. In the moon pool, Otter and the Skylars hung up their BCs, tanks, and regulators, and passed their fins and masks up to Drew, who was already inside. They climbed into the wet porch. On the way in, Ezzy had given a nod of thanks to Gertrude and Gandolf, who were stationed near the white gazebo as if guarding the entrance.

"How'd you like the swim-through?" Otter asked Luke.

"Awesome!"

"Ezzy?" Otter said.

"Loved it," she answered. "Except for the lionfish I saw coming out."

"Yeah," said Otter. "We'll have to go after that one another time."

"What do you think, Dad?" said Luke. "Isn't this cool?"

"It certainly is," replied Dr. Skylar. "I can't believe we're standing in air fifty feet down."

Ezzy waited, expecting her father to do his usual misquote of some saying or cliché. But instead, he stood staring in wonder at the moon pool and inside of the wet porch compartment.

They showered, dried off, and put on t-shirts that had been brought down earlier. Otter let Luke lead the tour for his father, adding a few technical details here and there. Afterward, they sat at the table and looked out one of the big viewports.

"Anyone for a snack?" asked Drew, pulling out a strange looking bumpy ball encased in red wrapping.

"Huh?" said Dr. Skylar looking at the thing.

"It's the pressure!" Luke blurted out. "Right?"

Drew nodded. "You got it." With a pair of scissors, he cut a hole in the wrapping. The bumpy ball instantly transformed into a regular old bag of candy-coated chocolates. "The air inside the bag was compressed by the high pressure down here so it created that weird ball. Once we let the air in... voila."

"The real problem is chips," Otter laughed. "Either they get smashed by the pressure or you poke a hole in the bag before bringing them down, but then they go stale."

They passed around the chocolates and watched as a group of snappers swam up to the viewport and stared in.

"Hey, the chocolate still tastes pretty good," said Ezzy. "Even down here in the land of bland."

The others laughed.

"Okay, folks," said Otter. "Time to head back up. Don't want to get into decompression time."

Ezzy and Luke shook their heads.

"Thanks for the visit," said Dr. Skylar. "Truly something we will never forget."

On the way out, the group stopped to say hello to Gertrude and Gandolf. The huge groupers swam to Otter and rubbed up against him before doing the same to Luke. Even with her regulator in, Ezzy couldn't help but laugh. The fish were bigger than her brother. With one on each side, Luke literally disappeared between them. It brought a whole new meaning to—a grouper sandwich.

Joined by Lola, who'd gone back to the surface during their visit inside, the group rose slowly. It reminded Ezzy of their last trip up. She swiveled around nervously, peering out into the surrounding blue water. *Where are the giant lionfish? Are they still out there or did the lionfish team already get them?*

At fifteen feet, the divers halted their ascent to do a safety stop. Ezzy continued to peer into the surrounding sea searching for anything big coming their way. After three minutes and no disruptions, they surfaced. Zhao and the captain helped the group into the boat and off with their gear.

A half hour later, after they'd had some water and packed up their equipment, the captain started the engine and Zhao released them from the mooring line.

"Hey, what about Drew?" asked Luke.

"A team is on its way out to join him to prepare for the next mission," replied Otter. "We're gonna head slightly north to deploy Professor Miller's sensor package. It should only take a few minutes so we're going to live-boat it."

Some ten minutes later, Ezzy and her family watched as Lola and Zhao geared up, jumped into the water, and were handed Professor Miller's instrument package. They gave the okay sign before flipping over and heading for the bottom.

The captain kept the engine running in neutral. Before long, Lola and Zhao popped up on the surface nearby. They swam to the boat and climbed aboard.

"All set," Lola told the group. "Strapped that baby on some rubble at the base of the reef about ninety feet down."

"Let's head in," Otter told the captain.

He nodded, put the boat in gear, pushed the throttle forward, and they headed for shore.

Ezzy stared at the glassy sea, thinking how different the day was. No goopy green water. No creepy giant lionfish. No sharks. *Sharks!* She'd forgotten all about sharks. Ezzy silently repeated her mantra: *I am not good fish food. I am especially not good shark food.* Then she wondered when she'd again get to SCUBA dive to a coral reef. She hoped it wouldn't be too long. Ezzy also wondered what had happened to the genetically altered lionfish. Had the team already gotten them? And what about Dr. Mudbourne? Had he died or was he out there somewhere?

*   *   *

Mission Poop Tracker

fter lunch at Sea Station headquarters, the
Smiths transformed into their stooped, hard-
of-hearing alter egos. Ezzy, Luke, and their
father accompanied them to the nearby Palm Bay Resort for phase two of mission poop tracker. Upon ar-
rival, Luke gently helped the Smiths exit the car and
handed each a cane. Ezzy shook her head. Once again,
he was laying it on heavy.

At the pace of a tortoise, Gracie and Phil led the
group into the resort's reception area.

"Sweetie pie," Gracie croaked to the receptionist
on duty. "Remember us? We came by the other day."

Ezzy watched to see if the young receptionist
would buy their over-the-top delivery. The girl had
purple hair and matching fingernail polish.

"Oh, of course," she answered. "Mrs. Jones, wasn't it?"

Gracie turned to Ezzy so the girl couldn't see and winked.

"That's right, honey" muttered Phil. "What a memory. What's your name again?"

She pointed to a badge. "Sasha."

"Of course," stuttered Phil. "I'd forget my own name if my lovely wife wasn't here to remind me."

"So true, sweetie," said Gracie. "We were wondering Sasha, if it wouldn't be too much trouble to show a room to our grandkids and their dad here." She turned to the Skylars.

Dr. Skylar waved awkwardly and tussled Luke's hair, while Ezzy stood nearby and smiled as innocently as possible.

"Sure," replied Sasha. "Let me see what rooms are available." She tapped on the keyboard on the desk. "Looks like room 212 is open. But I can't really leave the desk, let me see if I can find someone to take you up."

A lean man with windblown blonde hair wearing a dark blue polo shirt and well-pressed khakis entered the reception area. He smiled broadly at the group. "Is there something I can help with, Sasha?"

"Perfect timing," she replied. "This is our manager, Henry. This nice couple are the Joneses. They're thinking of staying with us next summer and would like to show a room to their family here. Room 212 is open.

Any chance you could show it to them?"

"Of course," he said. "Right this way."

Ezzy gave Luke a look to say here-we-go.

The group followed Henry into a nearby elevator. It took longer than usual as Phil and Gracie moved agonizingly slowly, playing up their disguises. They made small talk with Henry about where they were from and what they hoped to see on their next trip to the Keys. They repeatedly asked him to speak louder and appeared slightly confused. Ezzy knew it was all part of the act and the information they provided was total lies. *They are very good at this*, she thought.

Henry had an all-access keycard to unlock the room. Once inside, Gracie waved her arms about. "Just look at the view of the ocean and the nice-sized beds. It's just lovely. Don't you think, kids?"

"It sure is, *Grandma*," said Ezzy, laughing inside.

Luke raised his hand, crossed his legs, and fidgeted. "Uh, excuse me."

Ezzy rolled her eyes and whispered, "Don't overdo it."

"Yes?" said the manager.

"I have to like kinda go," said Luke sheepishly. "Can I use the bathroom?"

The man chuckled. "Sure, I think that'll be okay."

Luke ran into the bathroom. Minutes later Ezzy heard the toilet flush. Soon, she heard another flush.

Luke came out. "Whoo, so much better."

The others chuckled.

"You know, Henry," said Gracie. "If we do come, we might want to get one of your suites. Would it at all be possible to see one of those?"

Henry shrugged. "If one's available, sure. Let me call Sasha and check." He took out a cell phone and called the front desk.

Meanwhile, Ezzy saw Luke give Gracie and Phil the thumbs up.

"Okay, no problem," said Henry. "Follow me."

After another slow-motion walk to the elevator, they went up to the third floor. Henry unlocked another door and led them through. "This is the coconut suite," he said. "We have several more just like it. In addition to two bedrooms, there's also a fold-out couch in the sitting room."

A few minutes later as Henry was showing them a bathroom, Ezzy raised her hand. "Uh, excuse me, Sir."

"Yes?"

She tried to look embarrassed. "Is it okay if like I use the bathroom too?"

"What are you feeding these kids?" the man joked. "Sure."

"Thanks," said Ezzy. She closed the door and locked it. A small palm tree sat in the corner, and more decorated the towels. In place of a soap dish was a coconut shell. It held a coconut-shaped bar of soap.

From her pocket, Ezzy removed the small bag of

orange powder the Smiths had given her. She carefully emptied half into the toilet. The water immediately turned bright yellow. She chuckled. It looked like concentrated pee. Ezzy flushed, and the yellow water disappeared down the toilet. She repeated the exercise with the remaining dye powder and flushed a second time. Washing her hands, Ezzy noticed a few yellow spots on her shorts. She walked out and awkwardly tried to cover the spots with her hands.

"Better, honey?" asked Gracie eyeing her with interest.

"Yes, Grandma," said Ezzy smiling. "All set."

The rest of the visit was uneventful, and soon the Skylars and Smiths were headed back to Sea Station headquarters.

"Phase two of mission poop tracker complete," said Phil in the car.

"Now we wait to see if any of the dye comes out on the reef," added Gracie. "Professor Miller said it could take a few days."

Ezzy listened to the conversation while staring out the window. She liked being part of the Smiths' team and wondered if the dye would show up on the reef. As they drove over a small bridge, something caught Ezzy's eye. "Pull over!" she shouted.

Phil swerved the car onto the shoulder on the other side of the bridge.

"What's wrong?" asked Dr. Skylar. "Luke, are you feeling car sick?"

Luke shook his head. "Nope. Not me this time."

"In the canal," said Ezzy as she opened her door and jumped out, yelling back, "Come on."

The rest of the group exited the car and followed her to a low rock wall lining the small bridge. Below was the canal connecting Florida Bay to the Atlantic Ocean. The tide was flowing in and amid the water heading for Florida Bay were swirls and streaks of bright yellow.

"Whoa," said Luke. "Is that the dye?"

"It sure looks like it," answered Phil turning to his wife. "Right hon?"

"Definitely."

"What's it doing there?" asked Ezzy.

"Looks like the dye is coming from upstream," observed Dr. Skylar. "On the other side of the bridge."

Phil and Gracie stopped traffic so they could all safely cross the road to the other side of the bridge.

Ezzy pointed to the water. "There!"

"It's coming out of the wall," said Luke.

Ezzy thought so too. Just below the water, a narrow stream of bright yellow was flowing out from the limestone into the canal.

"Well," said Gracie. "They did say the underlying limestone was full of holes. Maybe more holes than they thought."

"We'd better report this to Otter when we get

back," said Phil, pulling out his phone to take a photo. "Wastewater entering the canal can't be good."

"Does this mean it's not coming out on the reef and causing the algae bloom?" asked Luke.

Phil scratched his chin. "Not sure. Some could still be flowing that way too. Guess we'll have to wait and see."

"Let's head back to the base," said Gracie. "Mission poop tracker is already producing excellent results."

As they got back into the car, Ezzy wondered if people at the resort were purposely dumping their wastes into the canal or if it was an innocent mistake. Either way, with their discovery, hopefully it would be fixed. Smiling to herself, Ezzy silently said: *Chock up another one for team Skylar-Smith and the planet.*

*   *   *

Once back at base, the group told Otter what they'd discovered and showed him the photo.

"I'll notify the authorities," said Otter. "Clearly whatever they're doing with their wastewater isn't right. And some could still be flowing out to the reefs."

A boat's horn sounded outside.

The group headed out. A motorboat with a Fish and Wildlife Service logo had pulled up to the dock.

"Yo, Otter," shouted Sam from the boat. "Got something for you."

Otter led the group down to the dock. "Hey, Sam. What's up?"

"Take a look in the pails in the stern."

Ezzy and the others walked along the dock to the boat's stern to look in the three large garbage pails on the deck.

"Whoa!" said Luke. "You got 'em."

Ezzy stared at what was inside the pails. Along with numerous small lionfish, were several of the giant mutant variety. "Are they dead? Like really dead?"

"Definitely dead," answered Sam.

"Where were they?" asked Otter.

"And how did you get them?" added Phil.

"Found the fish farm boat. Captain had some of the chemical attractant left. Also said he had nothing to do with what happened on the dock at the fish farm. He offered to help us get the fish. Stuff worked like a gem. Put it in the water and a little later those giant fish showed up along with a bunch of smaller ones."

"Did you get em all?" asked Ezzy.

"We think so."

"Any sign of Dr. Mudbourne?" Dr. Skylar asked.

Sam shook his head. "Nope, nothing."

Ezzy again wondered what had happened to the scientist. If he did survive the lionfish, which seemed nearly impossible, he'd probably already left the area. Hopefully she would never run into Dr. Mudbourne again. Even though her father seemed to think he wasn't all bad, Ezzy wasn't so sure.

"Hey Sam," said Otter. "Alec asked me about the fish farm this morning. What's going to happen to it now that Mudbourne is gone?"

"Tell Alec not to worry," he answered. "We're going to work with Justin to be sure it stays in business, minus the genetics lab. We're also going to find someone to replicate the remaining lionfish love potion. It could help us control the population."

"Could be something good that comes out of this after all," said Gracie.

Phil turned to the others and shook his head smiling. "Bright side."

"Uh, Sam," said Otter. "We've got something else for you to look into."

"You do?"

"Thanks to our crack investigative team here." He nodded to the group. "They discovered that wastewater from Palm Bay Resort is leaking into the nearby canal."

"Really?" said Sam. "Do you have proof?"

Phil took out his phone and showed the man the photo of the yellow dye in the canal and explained what they'd done. While they were talking, Ezzy heard a familiar sound. She walked down the dock so that she could see into the water behind the boat. A flat whiskered gray snout had just popped up. "Manatee!"

The group gathered beside Ezzy and watched as two manatees swam slowly down the canal toward the ocean.

"I love manatees," said Luke.

"You love all animals," noted Ezzy. "But you know what. I love manatees too."

"Me too," said Gracie.

"Me three," said Phil.

"Me four," added Dr. Skylar before turning to the Smiths. "Are you going to stay to see if Professor Miller's sensor detects the dye on the deep reef?"

Gracie turned to her husband. "We thought about sticking around, but we're thinking there's another adventure we'd like to do on the way home. Professor Miller will tell us if she detects anything out on the reef."

"Another adventure?" asked Ezzy, thinking maybe it was another investigation.

Phil grabbed his wife's hand. "We're going to do a swamp walk in the Everglades!"

Ezzy shook her head. "Whaat? There's alligators and snakes there, probably big spiders too."

"I know," said Gracie. "It's fantastic. We read they have fish-eating spiders. Crawl down trees and wiggle their legs in the water to attract fish and then... grab 'em."

"Yuck," moaned Ezzy.

"Awesome," said Luke.

"No, really," Phil said. "We read all about it and it's very safe. They do the swamp walk all the time, and it's especially good for photographers."

Ezzy shook her head vigorously. "Nope, never, not for me."

"I'd do it," said Luke.

"I have a better idea," said Dr. Skylar. "I was thinking, since we all love manatees so much, how about we take a little detour before going home. We could go up to Crystal River just north of Tampa and go snorkeling with the manatees."

"Now that sounds like a *good* idea," said Ezzy, nodding with enthusiasm.

"Yes, please," said Luke.

"Okay then," Dr. Skylar announced. "You two go hiking with the gators, and we'll swim with the manatees."

"Hey, maybe we can do both," said Gracie. "By the way, what's up for next year? Are you going on another Wonder List adventure?"

Ezzy turned to her father. "Dad, Luke and I have been talking. We want to see more of mom's Wonder List for sure, but we have another idea."

"You do?"

Luke nodded.

"People are really messing up the ocean, especially coral reefs," said Ezzy. "And... "

"Yeah," interrupted Luke. "Just on this trip we've

seen invasive species, pollution, and algae blooms."

"And don't forget climate change," Ezzy added. "We just think next year maybe we should do something to help."

Gracie smiled. "You've already done a lot, helping to stop wildlife smuggling in the Galápagos, preventing a meltdown of a glacier in Greenland, and our recent escapade here in the Keys."

Luke smiled. "But we want to do more."

"Like what?" asked their father.

Ezzy shrugged. "Not sure. But since we live near Washington, maybe we could get kids at school to visit Congress or write letters to the President to tell him we need to do more to protect the ocean and animals."

"And go on one of those trips where you help rescue sea turtles or something," offered Luke.

Their father hugged his two kids. "I think that is an excellent idea. We can put your mom's Wonder List on hold for a bit and come up with something wondrous in another way."

"Hey," said Gracie. "I love that idea. Count us in if you want company."

"Right you are, sugar plum," added Phil.

Suddenly, Dr. Skylar got a look on his face like he just remembered something. "Hey, I know something that might be just the thing."

"What?" asked Luke.

Ezzy didn't say anything, but thought, *wait for it.*

Her father winked and said, "You're gonna love it."

*   *   *

Note from the Author:
Real vs Made-Up

Twice in my life I've had the incredible opportunity to live underwater for one to two weeks in Aquarius Reef Base, the world's only operating undersea lab a couple miles off Key Largo, Florida. But before that, in between my junior and senior year in college, I had a summer job at the precursor to Aquarius—Hydrolab in St. Croix, USVI. I was a support or safety diver, which is another way of saying underwater servant. I delivered equipment, food, cleaned up inside the lab after missions, and was an all-around assistant. It was the best summer job ever. I learned about science, fieldwork, diving, and working as part of a team. I also spent two years as the Chief Scientist for Aquarius Reef Base. These programs hold fond memories for me and were a vital part of my early career, where I learned, got inspired, and was greatly encouraged. Thank you to all involved.

In this book, I based much of what happens on some of my favorite stories about living underwater and working in the ocean. As in the previous two books in the Wonder List Adventures, while parts of the story are based on real science, some of it is pure fiction. The characters are all fictitious, but some names may be familiar to those I've worked with. As for the story and science, see if you can tell what is real and what is made-up! Answers follow.

- **People living underwater are called aquanauts.**

- **Scientists can live underwater in an undersea laboratory to study coral reefs.**

- **The moon pool or hatchway can be left open fifty feet undersea, and the ocean doesn't flow in.**

- **Once a person is underwater for twenty-four hours or more their body becomes saturated with gas, much of it is nitrogen, and this can lead to nitrogen narcosis.**

- **When living underwater at high pressure, your taste buds don't work.**

- **Pizza and even a lemon meringue pie have been delivered underwater.**

- **When viewed at depths below about sixty feet, blood appears blue-green.**

- A cable system around Aquarius is like an underwater highway in case visibility gets bad and divers need to feel their way back to the lab.

- Nighttime on a coral reef can be very noisy.

- Visitors, including kids, can make a dive to the undersea lab during missions.

- Giant goliath groupers like to rub up against certain people.

- Goliath groupers create booms to scare away other fish.

- Lights turned on at night underwater create a food-web-in-action show.

- People living underwater must go through decompression before returning to the surface.

- Aquanauts sometimes do their business outside and fish love it.

- Someone once piped the music from the movie *Jaws* underwater on a hydrophone.

- Lionfish are invasive species in the waters off Florida.

- Genetically altered lionfish have been found in Florida and grow bigger than normal.

- The spines of a giant lionfish can scratch the acrylic viewports of the undersea lab.

- A chemical attractant produced from lionfish can help to attract them.

- People are trying to teach groupers and sharks to eat lionfish in tanks.

- Fish farm wastes are being used to grow sea vegetables.

- An algae is used as a thickener in ice cream.

- The ground in the Florida Keys is full of holes.

- Excess nutrients entering the ocean can cause algae blooms.

- It is dangerous to swim through algae blooms on regular SCUBA gear.

- The ground underlying Key Largo, FL is made up of an old coral reef that grew some 125,000 years ago.

- Satellite imagery of sea surface temperatures is only accurate for the top few centimeters of the ocean.

- The Gulf Stream creates cold and warm core swirling eddies.

- Someone once flushed dye down a toilet at a hotel in the Florida Keys, and it came out in a nearby canal.

- Someone once got hugged by a manatee while snorkeling at Crystal River.

- Pollution is causing sea grass to die and because of it, manatees are starving.

- There are fish-eating spiders in the Everglades swamp.

Real vs Made-Up Answers

- **People living underwater are called aquanauts.**
  Real. This is the underwater equivalent of astronauts.

- **Scientists can live underwater in an undersea laboratory to study coral reefs.**
  Real. Scientists living in the Aquarius Reef Base have six to nine hours a day to SCUBA dive down to 100 feet. They do surveys and experiments on coral, study fish, sponge, algae, and test underwater technology or collect data with special instruments. NASA also uses the undersea lab to train astronauts.

- **The moon pool or hatchway can be left open fifty feet undersea, and the ocean doesn't flow in.**
  Real. Just like in the book, the moon pool or open hatchway into the wet porch compartment can be left open if the air pressure inside Aquarius is kept equal to the seawater pressure outside. Water won't flow in.

- Once a person is underwater for twenty-four hours or more their body becomes saturated with gas, much of it is nitrogen, and this can lead to nitrogen narcosis.

  Real. Nitrogen narcosis can make people feel distracted or silly. It can make you laugh until you cry when watching a funny movie (I know from personal experience). But it does not affect everyone in the same way and is not a constant problem.

- When living underwater at high pressure your taste buds don't work.

  Real. For some reason that we don't completely understand, food tends to taste bland while living underwater in Aquarius Reef Base. I said that on-camera once and someone sent us a box of hot sauces.

- Pizza and even a lemon meringue pie have been delivered underwater.

  Real. During missions, a transfer pot is used by divers to bring equipment, clothes, and food to the habitat. Sometimes the aquanauts get special deliveries, including pizza and on one of my missions, a lemon meringue pie. It really did look and taste like a yellow-goo-white-slime pie.

- **When viewed at depths below about sixty feet, blood appears blue-green.**

  Real. One time while diving below sixty feet I cut my leg. When I looked down, it looked like I was bleeding blue-green blood. Aargh! Red light has a long wavelength. As sunlight enters the ocean from above, red light is absorbed before blue or green light. So... without artificial light below about sixty feet, things that are red really do appear blue-green.

- **A cable system around Aquarius is like an underwater highway in case visibility gets bad and divers need to feel their way back to the lab.**

  Real. During the week before a mission, aquanauts train on how to use specialized SCUBA gear and what to do if something goes wrong. This includes how to find your way back to safety if you cannot see due to poor visibility. You can feel on the cables for arrows that point back to the undersea lab. Once you have been down past the no-decompression limits you cannot go directly to the surface without getting the bends, which can be deadly. When living underwater, going directly to the surface is dangerous.

- **Nighttime on a coral reef can be very noisy.**

  Real. When going to sleep in the underwater lab, it can be surprisingly noisy outside. You hear a lot of snaps, pops, and crackles from shrimp, crabs, and other creatures on the surrounding reefs. I think the metal of the undersea lab makes it all sound louder.

- **Visitors, including kids, can make a dive to the undersea lab during missions.**

  Real. During my missions we had several visitors, including a high school student, a congresswoman, and a journalist from ABC's Good Morning America. They can only stay for a short time before doing a SCUBA dive back to the surface.

- **Giant goliath groupers like to rub up against certain people.**

  Real. There were two goliath groupers that liked to hang out around the undersea lab. They particularly liked to rub up against one of the staff when he was working outside. They became very friendly, and for their protection, we really did have a policy not to touch or hug the groupers.

- **Goliath groupers create booms to scare away other fish.**

  Real. Goliath groupers use their mouth and body to create loud booms underwater when startled or injured, to protect their territories and in courtship.

- **Lights turned on at night underwater create a food-web-in-action show.**

  Real. At night, lights turned on underwater attract zooplankton (small animals), which attract fish, which attract larger predators. We once saw a squid zoom past feeding and also a barracuda.

- **People living underwater must go through decompression before returning to the surface.**

  Real. Before returning to the surface, aquanauts must go through seventeen and a half hours of decompression, which entails slowly bringing the pressure inside the lab back to surface pressure. As in the story, the moon pool is shut and the pressure inside changed by the shore-based crew. But they also add an additional person inside who has not been living underwater to supervise and be sure everyone is okay. That was left out of the story.

- **Aquanauts sometimes do their business outside and fish love it.**

  Real. There is a toilet inside, but it tends to get clogged, and it is a small living space. So many aquanauts prefer the become one with the sea option. The fish do like to eat human wastes, which can be a little problem. And analysis has shown that the nutrients around the habitat are not any higher than in the surrounding water. The fish really are fat and happy.

- **Someone once piped the music from the movie *Jaws* underwater on a hydrophone.**

  Real. On my very first dive at night during a mission as a support diver at Hydrolab, in St. Croix, someone played a practical joke on me by putting the music from *Jaws* on the hydrophone and I could hear it. Kinda creepy!

- **Lionfish are invasive species in the waters off Florida.**

  Real. Lionfish are native to the Indian and Pacific Oceans. However, they are now found off Florida, in the Bahamas, Caribbean, and Gulf of Mexico. With no natural predators, they threaten native populations by eating lots of small crustaceans and fish. Lionfish tournaments are held to help

control the population and local restaurants even have it on their menu.

- **Genetically altered lionfish have been
found in Florida and grow bigger than
normal.**
Made-up. So far, no genetically altered
lionfish have been found. Lionfish normally
grow to less than two feet in length. Their
spines are toxic, and people do use Kevlar
gloves when handling them.

- **The spines of a giant lionfish can
scratch the acrylic viewports of the
undersea lab.**
Made-up. The viewports are made of
thick acrylic and cannot be scratched by
even large fish.

- **A chemical attractant produced from
lionfish can help to attract them.**
Made-up. So far, no one has created a
lionfish love potion. But if they could,
maybe it would help to catch them and
control the invasive population.

- **People are trying to teach groupers
and sharks to eat lionfish in tanks.**
Real and Made-up. Some people are trying
to teach groupers and sharks in the wild
to eat lionfish, but I don't know of anyone

trying to do it in tanks. So far, it hasn't really worked.

• **Fish farm wastes are being used to grow sea vegetables.**

   Real. Some aquaculture facilities or fish farms use their wastes to fertilize and grow plants, including "sea vegetables" like Purslane that can grow in saltwater. I visited an aquaculture facility like this run by Mote Marine Laboratory in Sarasota, Florida. Purslane does in fact taste a little bit like salty, crunchy spinach.

• **An algae is used as a thickener in ice cream.**

   Real. Red algae is used to help thicken ice cream, but you cannot taste it.

• **The ground in the Florida Keys is full of holes.**

   Real. The ground underlying much of the Florida Keys is made of limestone and it has a lot of holes in it. Saltwater from the ocean can flow into the ground (think rising sea level) and fresh groundwater can flow out, including coming out at the seafloor in the ocean.

• **Excess nutrients entering the ocean can cause algae blooms.**

Real. Too much phosphorous or nitrogen can act like fertilizer in the ocean and cause algae to grow rapidly and in abundance, causing a bloom.

- **It is dangerous to swim through algae blooms on regular SCUBA gear.**

  Made-up. But maybe. It would depend on the extent, density, and type of algae involved in a bloom. In most cases, it is safe to swim through an algae bloom on SCUBA.

- **The ground underlying Key Largo, FL is made up of an old coral reef that grew some 125,000 years ago.**

  Real. Some 125,000 years ago sea level was about fifteen feet higher than today. A coral reef grew, and when sea level fell, the limestone that made up the reef became much of the land we know as the Florida Keys.

- **Satellite imagery of sea surface temperatures is only accurate for the top few centimeters of the ocean.**

  Real. Using sensors aboard satellites we can estimate the temperature of the ocean. But it is only the temperature of the very surface or top few centimeters.

- **The Gulf Stream creates cold and warm core swirling eddies.**

  Real. Swirling patches of water that break off the Gulf Stream are called cold and warm core eddies. You get warm core eddies to the north and cold core eddies to the south of the current.

- **Someone once flushed dye down a toilet at a hotel in the Florida Keys, and it came out in a nearby canal.**

  Real. No names shall be given, but this did happen, and it was discovered that the hotel's wastewater was seeping out into a local canal.

- **Someone once got hugged by a manatee while snorkeling at Crystal River.**

  Real. The someone was me and it was fantastic. I was snorkeling with manatees at Crystal River, Florida and one swam up to me and hugged me. I was laughing so hard I spit out my snorkel. They are surprisingly strong and very cute. I loved it!

- **Pollution is causing sea grass to die and because of it, manatees are starving.**

  Real. Unfortunately, this is true, especially on the east coast of Florida. Poor water quality, excess nutrients, and algae blooms have killed the sea grass, which is the main source of food for manatees. People are working to restore the sea grass and improve water quality, but we need to do more ASAP.

- **There are fish-eating spiders in the Everglades swamp.**

  Real. I went on a swamp walk in the Everglades from famous photographer Clyde Butcher's shop. I saw a couple of alligators but felt safe with my guide. He told me about fish-eating spiders, but we didn't see any or any snakes. It was super cool.

Youth Ocean Conservation Organizations

If you are interested in getting involved with ocean conservation or science, be sure to check out your local aquarium or nature centers or visit one while away from home. And here are a few organizations to look into as well:

- Youth Ocean Conservation Summit: http://www.yocs.org
- Earth Echo International: https://www.earthecho.org
- The Ocean Project: https://theoceanproject.org/youth/
- Sea Youth Rise UP: http://seayouthriseup.org
- Ocean Advocates: https://oceanconservationtrust.org/about/ocean-advocates/

If you are interested in a career in marine science or ocean education, check out these websites for more information:

- Sea Grant's Marine Careers: https://www.marinecareers.net
- VIMS The Bridge: https://masweb.vims.edu/bridge/
- NOAA Education: https://www.noaa.gov/education
- National Marine Educators Association: https://www.marine-ed.org

Acknowledgments

Just like working undersea, it takes a team to create and publish a book. My sincere thanks to the wonderful team at Tumblehome books, especially publisher and editor, Penny Noyce. Appreciation to the rest of the group as well, including Rebecca Raibley, Yu-Yi Ling, and Barnas Monteith. Once again, illustrator Tammy Yee created an extraordinary cover, map, and a diagram of the undersea lab. WOW and thank you.

For their inspiration, hugely helpful feedback, and time, big hugs and thanks to all my test readers, including Susan Tate, Cristina Veresan, student Izzy Hesse, and Debbi and Olivia Stone.

Deep (pun intended) gratitude also goes to the staff and all the colleagues I worked with over the years at Hydrolab and Aquarius Reef Base. You made me laugh, taught me so much, and were an inspiration. Thank you for your support, training, friendship, and lots of great stories. I could not have written this book without you and my time spent amid the fishes.

A note of thanks to Dr. Kevan Main for a fascinating tour of Mote Marine Lab's aquaculture facility in Sarasota, Florida and discussion about fish farming and growing of sea vegetables using the wastestream.

And lastly, there's another team that needs a big thanks. That's my ever-present family and friends who laugh at my jokes, encourage me, and provide a wealth of moral support. Special thanks to Linda and Dave for laughing when I read or send them story parts, and for their never-ending encouragement. Dave, you continue to amaze me with your warmth, kindness, love, and of course, an infinite supply of tears-producing humor. We make a great team.

About The Author

Dr. Ellen Prager is a marine scientist and author, widely recognized for her expertise and ability to make science entertaining and understandable for people of all ages. She currently works as a freelance writer, consultant, Chief Scientist for Storm Center Communications, and science advisor to Celebrity Cruises in the Galapagos Islands. She was previously the Chief Scientist for the Aquarius Reef Base program in Key Largo, Florida and the Assistant Dean at the University of Miami's Rosenstiel School of Marine and Atmospheric Science. Dr. Prager has built a national reputation as a scientist and spokesperson, serving as a consultant for the Disney movie *Moana* and appearing on The Today Show, Good Morning America, CBS Early Show, CNN, Fox News, The Weather Channel, and Discovery Channel. She is the author of numerous popular science books and the successful *Tristan Hunt and the Sea Guardians* series of middle-grade adventure novels.